Bolan wondered where the hell they had come from

The Executioner looked to his right as he saw nearly a dozen well-armed soldiers advancing on his position. The muzzles of their weapons winked erratically, but there was one massive sound of destruction from their combined reports. Bolan narrowly escaped being ventilated, getting low and listening to the familiar sounds of bullets zinging over his head or striking the wooden outbuilding.

He realized it had been a trap. Several times already he'd been a target, and now he was being hunted. But instead of tracking him, they had waited until he'd come to them.

It was likely that a lot more people would die if the Executioner didn't make a move.

MACK BOLAN ®
The Executioner

The Executioner

Don Pendleton's®

ENTRY POINT

THE CARNIVORE PROJECT 1

A GOLD EAGLE BOOK FROM
WORLDWIDE®

TORONTO • NEW YORK • LONDON
AMSTERDAM • PARIS • SYDNEY • HAMBURG
STOCKHOLM • ATHENS • TOKYO • MILAN
MADRID • WARSAW • BUDAPEST • AUCKLAND

First edition June 2005
ISBN 0-373-64319-5

Special thanks and acknowledgment to
Jon Guenther for his contribution to this work.

ENTRY POINT

Printed in U.S.A.

Man does not enter the battle to fight, but for victory. He does everything he can to avoid the first and obtain the second.

—Ardant du Picq 1821–1870

I walk a path behind terrorists so others don't have to. I walk that path willingly. I walk with swift force, iron resolve and the will to take the offensive. These are the key elements of victory.

—Mack Bolan

For those in the trenches of electronic warfare,
working behind the scenes to keep America secure.
Live Large

Prologue

Washington, D.C.

No one heard the shot and no one saw the shooter.

Dr. Mitchell Fowler felt the sniper's bullet, an excruciating burning and tearing sensation as the slug ripped through his aorta and blew a hole out his back. Barely after his body hit the ground—a matter of seconds—he died.

The only way people around him even knew anything was wrong was due to the way Fowler's body slammed into the steel-and-concrete facade of the metro FBI offices. That, coupled with the blood that stretched hot, red fingers away from the pool forming under his twitching corpse, made it evident that someone had shot him. With the exception of a couple of agents, the rest of the group scattered for whatever cover they could find.

The agents started yelling in the direction of a tourist group, screaming at the driver to get everybody back on the bus, and to do it "right goddamn now!" They then produced firearms from beneath their jackets and went prone on the sidewalk, staying far enough from the body to prevent injury from ricochets or follow-up shots. The agents looked in all directions. Their eyes roved the street corners and tops of buildings for any telltale sign that might betray the shooter:

sunlight on metal, movement, noise. The effort proved futile, given the screaming and panicked bystanders who were running in any direction that might take them away from the horrific sight.

Agent Mark Sheaghan, who had just been coming off duty for the day, crawled toward Fowler's body. He checked the man's pulse at neck and wrist. Nothing. Sheaghan wasn't surprised, considering the amount of blood. He whispered a few brief words of respect to the fallen man, then met another agent's eyes and shook his head in response to the expectant gaze.

It had been a few years since something like this had happened in Washington, D.C., when someone had gone around the city and outlying areas blowing holes in innocent people with a high-power assault rifle. But someone had just had the balls to shoot a federal scientist in front of his own office building, and Sheaghan couldn't help but wonder if that nightmare was about to start all over again.

SHE TRIED TO HOLD BACK her tears as she called her mother and said goodbye.

Someone had altered Tyra MacEwan's life, and if she were ever able to come out of hiding, she would find out who was responsible and kill that individual. After all, she was pretty proficient with a gun. Her daddy, having been a Texas rancher all of his life, had made it plain he wanted his little girl to know how to defend herself, especially if she was going to live alone in the big, mean city of Boston.

Shortly after she'd left for the Massachusetts Institute of Technology, her father died of a heart attack while out roping. Her trip was short-lived, having to come home and bury her father, but MacEwan wasn't the type to give up easily. Her mother always told her she'd inherited her father's stubborn ways, and that he was as bullheaded as the animals he'd worked with most of his life. God, how she missed him and wished he were with her in this whole, crazy mess.

"When are you coming back, dear?" her mother asked her.

"I don't know yet, Mom," she replied, fighting to keep her voice from shaking. "It may be awhile."

"Well, why are they sending you now? My goodness, Tyra, it's practically the middle of the night. What time is it there, anyway?"

MacEwan glanced at the green-blue numbers of the clock. Tears were streaking her vision as the windshield wipers cleared the steady rain.

"Just shy of two a.m.," she replied.

"Where are they sending you?"

"I can't tell you that, Mom. You know some of what I do and where I go is classified." The city looked eerie at that time of night, the thunder, lightning and chilly weather adding a dark foreboding to the circumstances. "Listen, Mom, I have to go or I'll miss my plane. I promise to call you as soon as I'm settled."

"Well, all right. You have a good trip but be careful, sweetheart."

"I will, Mom. I love you."

"I love you, too."

MacEwan disconnected the call and dropped the cell phone on the seat next to her. She felt lost. She couldn't take any public transportation—that was too risky. She did have a few friends she could have called and asked for a place to stay, but that would have resulted in a lot of uncomfortable questions, not to mention putting them in danger.

After all, someone had already killed Mitch, and it would be some time before the FBI found out who pulled the trigger—if ever. She wasn't willing to take a chance with anyone she cared about.

No, it was best for her to go it alone. It made sense to leave Washington. She'd get far enough away to make it difficult for anyone to find her, but not far enough that she couldn't keep an eye on the situation. There was a great threat looming on the horizon—a threat to her country—and she couldn't trust anyone else with the information. It was amazing that of all the people she had worked side by side with for all of those years now seemed untrustworthy to her.

But what choice did she have? Mitch was dead, and aside from him, she was the only one who knew what was going on. That made her indispensable to her country, and a threat to whomever was behind the security breach. One way or another, she had to find out who and why. Once she could prove that, then she would step forward and report it to the proper authorities, and they could do something about it.

Until then, the entire stability of the country's electronic network hung in the balance of a technological threat so unthinkable that MacEwan didn't know if she could find the answer in time.

She wondered if there was anyone on the face of the whole damn planet who could help her.

1

Mack Bolan knew he was being followed, and he suspected the four men in the unmarked sedan weren't a welcoming committee.

Two days had passed since his summons by the Man, with Harold Brognola serving as liaison. Meeting the President of the United States face-to-face was never Bolan's first choice, but he'd done it at Brognola's request, and because the Man expressed personal gratitude to the Executioner for making this exception.

Somehow the gunning down of an FBI scientist named Mitchell Fowler and the subsequent disappearance of ranch girl turned IT security expert were connected. At least, that was Barbara Price's take on it. Bolan had learned long ago to trust the intuition of Stony Man's beautiful and brilliant mission controller.

The assignment was supposed to be simple. Bolan was to pose as a new DOD information systems contractor for the Defense Advanced Research Projects Agency where the missing IT expert, Tyra MacEwan, had worked, and find out what happened to her.

"Simultaneously," Brognola added during their meeting

with the President, "you may help us get closer to whoever was responsible for the death of Dr. Fowler."

Naturally, because Fowler's murder had been such a public spectacle, procedure called for it to be handled by federal agencies in a public fashion. But the general public didn't know about the disappearance of Tyra MacEwan, so the President was able to involve Stony Man Farm.

Yeah, so it was somehow important to the Man, who really didn't say much during the meeting. Brognola was caught between a rock and a hard place. It was impractical to send in Able Team for something like this. Bolan could wade through DARPA politics much less conspicuously than three hard-nosed vets led by the fiery Carl Lyons. There *were* parts of the mission that were better suited to the peculiar talents of that threesome, but the Executioner's gut told him to take the gig—it was an instinct that had saved his life more times than he could count.

It was the same instinct that alerted him to the tail. They had been following him for about an hour as he drove toward DARPA. Bolan immediately sensed the danger, but he was simultaneously perplexed by it. At most, a dozen individuals knew about the Fowler-MacEwan connection, and only half that many would have any knowledge of Bolan's involvement. For someone to have picked up his tail so quickly confirmed his suspicion that the missing woman was important to more than just Stony Man and the Oval Office.

Bolan checked the rearview mirror and watched as the tail car followed him off the exit from Interstate 66. That was another oddity; they didn't seem too interested in remaining inconspicuous. Then again, that was a good sign they were going to make their move soon.

The soldier reached beneath the seat and withdrew his trusted .44 Magnum Desert Eagle. As he stopped for the light at the interchange, the sedan stopped immediately behind him, and all but the driver exited the vehicle. Even in the twilight, the Executioner could clearly see the hardware in their hands. He first looked ahead of him—there was nowhere to evade in the rush-hour traffic without endangering innocents. Bolan reacted immediately, ducking in his seat as the trio raised their machine pistols and opened up with a brutal salvo. Fortunately, the SUV belonged to Stony Man Farm. While the vehicle exterior appeared normal, key areas of the body and frame were reinforced with Kevlar. A steel blast plate across the bottom and sides of the gas tank prevented the accelerant effects of bombs. Bolan's forethought in deciding to take the vehicle rather than settling for a standard rental saved his life.

The Executioner heard the enemy bullets strike the car, the sound reverberating through the roomy interior. He waited for a lull in the shooting before sliding across the seat and exiting on the passenger side. The Desert Eagle boomed in the twilight air as Bolan replied to his attackers with full fury. His would-be assassins obviously weren't ready for his appearance, because he got the closest one on the passenger side with a head shot before the other two could react. The round busted the man's skull apart and splattered blood and brain matter everywhere.

Bolan's second .44 slug hit the chest of the gunman who had exited from the rear passenger door of the sedan. The man's body twisted at a gross angle, and his chin slammed against the roof of the sedan before he fell to the pavement.

The remaining gunman and the driver obviously realized that in mere seconds their enemy had narrowed the odds by half. The gunner split away from the sedan on foot, and the driver decided not to wait around and be killed. He put the sedan in reverse, backing away from the situation with a squeal of tires. Unfortunately for a woman exiting from the interstate and slowing for the traffic light, the driver practically destroyed the front of her sports car. The little turbocharged, four-cylinder engine was no match for the heavy trunk of the sedan. The two vehicles collided in a deafening crash of crumpled metal and broken glass.

Bolan rushed to pursue the gunner on foot as the driver of the sedan leaped from his car and pulled a pistol. The soldier leveled the Desert Eagle on the run and triggered two rounds designed more to keep the driver's head down than to actually take him down. As it turned out, the second round ripped a furrow in the driver's shoulder, knocking the pistol from his hand.

With the shooter disarmed, Bolan turned his attention to the last guy, who had reached a vehicle in the cross traffic now stopped for the light. The Executioner cursed himself for not taking out the priority threats first, but the driver's reaction had thrown his plan just a bit. Bolan watched as the gunman yanked a terrified woman from her car—but he wasn't nearly as concerned about her as he was the infant in a car seat visible through the rear passenger door window.

Bolan realized his enemy hadn't seen the infant, and he decided that whatever went down, he had to protect the innocents. The soldier slowed as he approached the vehicle, the woman screaming as the man yanked her from the car and waved the gun at her head. Bolan could see he was Middle Eastern, short, lithe and wearing the all too familiar expression of a fanatic.

He was a terrorist, plain and simple.

Bolan adjusted his aim as the man began to scream at him in what sounded like Arabic—the Executioner stopped but he didn't lower his weapon. The man continued shouting as Bolan simply watched, willing himself to remain calm as the terrorist jammed the barrel of the machine pistol to the woman's head. Bolan's eyes flicked to the infant once more before he decided it was time to act.

Bolan squeezed the trigger.

The bullet hit dead center on the frame of the machine pistol, ripping through the casing, rendering the weapon useless, the impact driving it from the terrorist's grip. The woman looked as surprised as the gunman, but she had enough control to tear away from the man when he loosened his grip. It was Bolan's opening and he took it. The Executioner fired once more, this bullet punching through the terrorist's throat and cervical spine. The man's head rolled forward before his corpse dropped to the ground.

Bolan rushed to the body and frisked it for identification. The mother had moved to the passenger side and was now retrieving her infant. She looked intently at the Executioner a moment.

"It's okay," he said quietly. "You're safe now. I'm not going to hurt you."

The woman didn't say anything, but some of the fear and terror dissipated from her expression as she hugged the crying infant to her body.

Bolan left the area immediately, returning to the other two bodies and searching them as well. The driver was gone, having abandoned his sedan and left on foot. The soldier also searched the vehicle; just as with the three bodies, he found nothing that identified them. He did, however, find a matchbook stuck inside a pack of cigarettes that may have been a clue. He'd have to run it by Stony Man. If anyone could figure it out, Aaron "The Bear" Kurtzman could.

Bolan returned to his vehicle and quickly got away from the scene of carnage. Without a doubt, one of the bystanders who witnessed the shootout had already called it in over a cell phone, which meant the police would have a BOLO for his vehicle. He sure as hell couldn't drive through town without attracting attention—he needed to ditch the vehicle and find a suitable replacement.

And he already knew exactly where to go.

NICK'S AUTOMOTIVE WAS more than it appeared: a little unobtrusive auto mechanic's garage bordering the industrial area of Arlington. Bolan didn't know the owner's real name and Nicholas Smith—whose nickname was "Nookie" for his eclectic taste in women—had no idea who the Executioner was. That worked for both of them. Bolan *did* know that Nookie was an autobody guy in the Witness Protection Program for rendering testimony to put down a major car-theft ring being run by business concerns tied to organized crime. Not only was Nookie a first-class body man, but he was also a genius mechanic and reliable contact. He helped out now and then, made a little extra cash on the side for his trouble and didn't ask any questions.

Nookie stood, arms folded, and stared at the SUV. He finally shook his head with a lopsided grin and said, "It appears someone doesn't like you too much."

Bolan nodded. "Yeah, I've grown fairly used to that."

"I'm sure," Nookie replied with a chuckle.

"How long to fix it?"

He began circling the SUV, studying it with professional consideration. When he'd made one full inspection, he turned and smiled at Bolan. "Three days at most. Understand it's not that the damage is all that bad, but I'm going to have repaint it…after I patch and sand these holes. The primer needs at least twelve hours to cure, and another twenty-four for the paint to dry."

"Fine. You have something else I can use in the meantime?"

Nookie nodded. "As a matter of fact, I do. Follow me."

Bolan retrieved his clothing and hardware from the back of the SUV, and then followed the mechanic into another area of the garage where a woman sat leaning against a workbench. She had a bouffant hairdo, and wore pink hot pants and a loose-fitting sweater. She held a lit cigarette between her fingers, and when she saw Bolan, her expression changed from that of frustrated impatience to sensual interest.

Nookie said, "Hey, Tina, why don't you take a walk."

The woman tossed him a haughty, offended look before stubbing out her cigarette and walking away with a steady clop-clop of her three-inch spike heels. Nookie tossed a knowing look at Bolan, then snatched a dustcover from one of several covered vehicles parked in that area of the garage.

He smiled as he revealed the car. It was a luxury sedan, sort of a gold-bronze color, and fully loaded with leather interior. The thing was a boat, sure, but Bolan knew it would suit him perfectly. It wasn't so nice that he'd raise suspicions driving it, but it spelled success enough to assist his cover as a Defense contractor.

"This will work," Bolan said after a cursory inspection.

Nookie nodded and handed the Executioner the keys. "Take good care of her." As Bolan tossed his bag in back and got behind the wheel, Nookie jerked his thumb in the direction of the SUV and added, "Try not to bring her back with any of that business."

"I'll keep it in mind," Bolan said.

Nookie raised the garage door, and Bolan was soon headed toward the central area of Arlington and the DARPA offices. He pulled a cell phone from his jacket and dialed the Farm. Aaron Kurtzman answered almost immediately in his usual voice, which was a gruff and bold as his wrestlerlike physique. The Executioner thought of the big guy sitting in his wheelchair, hunkered over a computer terminal or some other sort of computer output.

"Hey, Striker. What's the good word?"

"I've got a word, but I'm afraid it's not good."

"What happened?" Kurtzman asked.

"I ran into some trouble shortly after I got here."

"What kind of trouble?"

"The kind speaking Arabic and toting machine pistols," Bolan replied. "Is the top dog around?"

"Yeah, wait one." Kurtzman would know from the way Bolan phrased the question that he thought they were being monitored. Not only would he get Brognola, but he would also activate all security and monitoring measures to assure a secure connection between them. Kurtzman came back twenty seconds later and said, "We're totally clean, Striker."

Brognola's voice came on the line, and he didn't sound the least bit happy. "Striker, you all right?"

"I'm alive, but I've got the distinct feeling someone's on to me."

"I don't see how that's possible. We've been very careful about this. We heard about the trouble in Arlington already—

police reports came in about ten minutes ago. We just weren't sure you were involved until you called. What the hell happened?"

Bolan explained it to the Stony Man chief, giving him only the pertinent details. Neither man had time for war stories; it wasn't the Executioner's practice to be long-winded about his activities anyway. While the Oval Office didn't necessarily like it, and Bolan had repeatedly turned down Brognola's offers to return to Stony Man as a full-fledged member, the Executioner was a free agent. He wasn't disposed to report his actions to Brognola or anybody else, but there was another reason he'd called, and he expressed that concern in no uncertain terms.

"I think Stony Man's security has been compromised," Bolan said.

"That's not possible," Brognola said.

"Come on, Hal. Nobody else knew about this except those in the loop. How could Arab terrorists have identified me so easily and then gone to the trouble of trying to kill me on top of that?"

"I'm not sure."

"Me neither, but I'm sure it wasn't coincidence or mistaken identity. Maybe they didn't know who I was, but they knew I was coming to Arlington and they considered me a threat."

"What makes you think we're dealing with Arab terrorists?"

"Speaking Arabic and carrying machine pistols fit the profile."

"Yes, I'd say that clinches it well enough," Brognola replied. "And it confirms our suspicion that terrorists were probably involved in Fowler's murder. What it doesn't tell us is how Tyra MacEwan's disappearance is tied to that."

"I think that my contact at DARPA may be able to shed some light on that," Bolan replied.

"Oh yeah, which reminds me," Brognola said. "I hate to spring a change of plans, but the person we originally had in place to meet you was sent out of the country on an emergency. His spot is being personally filled by the office director, Dr. Malcolm Shurish."

"He's Arabic?"

"Pakistani, to be correct, but everything Barb and Bear's contacts could pull on him says he's on our side."

"Well, as long as I play the part right, there shouldn't be any trouble. Listen, Hal, I'm pulling up on the DARPA offices now, so I'm going to have to break off, but let me speak to Bear a second."

"I'm here, Striker," Kurtzman's voice resounded. "What do you need?"

Bolan retrieved the matchbook he'd found in the terrorist vehicle and held it to the light of the dash in order to read it. "I need you to run a name for me…it's Riyad Bari, that's two words." He spelled it.

"What the heck does that mean?" Kurtzman asked.

"I don't know—that's what I need you to run through your databases and let me know next time I call. I found it written on the outside of a matchbook cover."

"All right, I'll get on it pronto. Hey, Striker?"

"Yeah?"

"You watch yourself. I don't have a real good feeling about any of this."

"Will do. Out here."

Bolan broke the connection, stored the cell phone in the glove compartment, exited the luxury sedan and adjusted his tie in the reflection in the car window under the parking lot lights before making his way to the front doors. It was after hours, but he had clearance and credentials, and he knew they were expecting him—whoever *they* were. Bolan wished he'd had time to prepare for the change in contacts, but this was the game and he'd agreed to play it. There was no point in complaining about it now.

Once he'd been cleared by security, a nice-looking brunette with long legs led Bolan to a waiting room outside the office of the director. He took the time to break out some information from the briefcase; it was just for show—the briefcase— but the file was quite real. He would be working for the Information Processing Technology Office, just one of the many divisions that comprised DARPA. Bolan was posing as Matthew Cooper, a former Defense systems contractor with the academic and work credentials that made him a perfect candidate for the job. Since the chief direction of research and special projects at DARPA were driven by the needs of the Department of Defense, Bolan's military background would also help him with the general environment.

So the Executioner would somehow find a way to be comfortable in his role, and hope that Stony Man's arrangement that he be left strictly alone to work on those things of his choosing would allow him the room he needed to find out why Tyra MacEwan had disappeared, and what that had to do with a sniper killing Fowler outside the offices of the single largest law-enforcement service in the world.

The door to the director's office opened and Bolan turned expectantly. The man was well dressed and wore more rings than a jewelry-store mock-up. He had dark skin with the faintest hint of a mustache and goatee, and was short and stocky.

"Mr. Cooper?" the man said, stepping forward with a smile. "I am Dr. Shurish. Welcome to the IPTO."

As Bolan stood to shake hands with the man, the world around him exploded in a collage of blinding light and deafening noise.

2

It felt to Mack Bolan like his teeth loosened from his gums as the concussion lifted him off his feet and slammed him against the wall. He had managed to get the briefcase in front of himself, so it absorbed the majority of the impact, preventing his head from being crushed against the wall. The bomb exploded with enough force to blow out the glass windows, but Bolan somehow managed to avoid the full effect.

The same couldn't be said for the secretary who had led Bolan to the waiting room. The bomb had obviously been planted directly under her desk, and she took the brunt. The concussion separated those shapely legs from her body, and the blast seared her skin. Through the murkiness enveloping the Executioner's mind, he could hear her tortured screams, although he couldn't actually see the woman. The screaming abruptly stopped.

Malcolm Shurish seemed to have fared better. As the dust and debris settled, the Executioner could see through the haze that the scientist was on his knees, bleeding from his forehead and lip—but at least he was conscious and breathing.

Bolan shook the stinging sensation from his eyes and felt something warm on his forehead as he wiped sweat from it.

He looked down and saw that a small splinter of wood had lodged in the back of his hand. He was bleeding but not badly. He could take care of it soon enough; for the moment it was more important to assist in evacuating any bystanders. The Executioner took a quick internal inventory, moving slowly but steadily, and convinced nothing was broken he climbed to his feet. He went quickly to Shurish and grabbed the scientist by his suit coat, hauling him to his feet. The man stopped in his tracks, resisting Bolan's urges for them to get out of the building.

"What about Cheryl?"

Bolan looked in the direction of the secretary's desk. The grisly site was a quick study. Her lower body was gone, the upper torso burned to the point that she was nothing more than a lump of flesh, almost inhuman and unrecognizable. There was the faintest hint of burned flesh and death, but the smell of gasoline and some other scent—something vaguely familiar—assaulted Bolan's nostrils and nearly overpowered him.

"She's gone," the Executioner said. "And now we need to go."

Bolan hustled Shurish through the office doors and got him outside to fresher air. The Executioner knew the place was soon to be swarming with emergency services personnel, including cops who were bound to ask a lot of uncomfortable questions he couldn't answer. Of course, that would only be until the FBI arrived. Bolan couldn't afford that kind of attention, but he also couldn't afford to leave. While running away might have seemed like a natural response to most, it would only make him more of a target. No, it was best to stay put and play it out. The priority now was to call Brognola before the cops got to him.

Once they were in the lobby, the fire alarms began to sound. Security guards assisted the pair outside and then returned to the building to assist other personnel.

Bolan insured Shurish was okay without assistance and then trotted to his car and retrieved his cell phone. He moved away from the area, dialing the Farm's number even as he heard the approach of sirens. It rang twice before Kurtzman picked up.

"I need to talk to Hal and pronto," Bolan said.

Brognola was on the line in a moment. "We've got more trouble," Bolan said.

"What's wrong?"

"Bomb just blew at the DARPA offices, and almost took out both me and Shurish. His secretary bought it. I think the bomb was beneath her desk."

"Damn," Brognola said. "All right, just hang tight. I'm going to have Barb get Able out there immediatcly to help. You hurt?"

"Not seriously," Bolan replied. "And for the time being, it's better if you keep the guys where they're at. I'll handle this. The FBI's going to be sniffing around pretty quick as it is, and the more unnecessary faces the worse it could get, particularly if I'm right about Stony Man's security being compromised. I'm more concerned about this bomb."

"What do you mean?"

"Well, as soon as the FBI forensic work starts to come in, have Bear go to work on it right away. I'm positive gasoline was used, but there was something else in it...something I've smelled before. I just can't place it right now."

"All right. We'll get to work on it right away," Brognola said.

"Okay, put Bear on."

"Good luck, Striker."

Kurtzman came on the line immediately. "This is a real eye-opener."

"Give it to me."

"That name is actually Arabic. *Riyad Bari* is Garden of Allah."

"Is there any significance to it?"

"A lot. Looks like you stumbled onto something pretty big. The Garden of Allah is actually a club here in D.C. It's on the south side of the city, and is long suspected of being a haven for members of the New Islamic Front."

A knot formed in Bolan's gut, and it felt as if his neck hairs stood on end. The NIF was a terrorist group that had recently penetrated the United States. According to the latest intelligence, it was planning something big, but its infrastructure was such that a joint task force of federal agencies under the Office of Homeland Security was having a tough time figuring out just what that *something* was.

The President had asked Brognola to start looking into it. The Executioner had been in regular contact with Hal Brognola, working any angles and leads he could come up with, but to no real avail. This latest piece of news was quite probably the break he'd been waiting for.

"I'll check it out as soon as I'm clear here."

"Hey," a voice said behind Bolan.

The Executioner felt a hand grab his shoulder, and he reacted out of reflex. He spun inward as he wrapped his left arm around the right arm of the speaker. He brought back his right hand, still holding the cell phone. He was prepared to deliver a smash to the throat, but stopped when he saw it was one of the security guards. The guy raised his free hand and winced in pain as Bolan had exerted considerable pressure on the man's elbow.

The Executioner immediately released him. "Sorry. I'm a little jumpy," he said.

"It's okay, sir," the guard replied. He was a younger man, and made his best attempt at a cordial smile while rubbing his elbow. "I guess now I know not to sneak up on you. I was just going to ask you not to use your cell phone until the bomb unit has cleared the area. It might set off additional explosives."

"Of course, you're right." Bolan made a show of turning it off. "I promise I won't use it again."

"I'm afraid I'll have to confiscate it for the duration of the emergency, sir."

"Not without a top-secret security clearance," the Executioner replied.

The young man reached into the breast pocket of his uniform shirt and yanked a security badge from it. It had a top-secret clearance stamped on the card, authorized and signed by both the director of the FBI and the Secretary of Defense. Bolan sighed as he handed the phone over to the younger man. It didn't matter that he'd called the Farm twice, since the minute it was shut off the memory was erased and data shredded such that even the brightest wouldn't have been able to hack through it.

"Thank you, sir. Now, I would suggest you go wait with the rest of the building's occupants until someone can speak with you."

Bolan nodded, put on his best scientist face and headed toward the crowd gathering on the other side of the parking lot.

Stony Man Farm, Virginia

BARBARA PRICE POURED herself some coffee, then dropped a pile of printouts and folders on her desk before sitting in her chair, closing her eyes and leaning her head back with a sigh. From what Kurtzman had told her upon her return from a meeting with the deputy director of the NSA, Price knew things couldn't get much worse.

Within the course of two hours, Mack Bolan had twice beaten the odds and escaped with his life. That was not the path of an ordinary man. Then again, the Executioner was not *just* an ordinary man—he was an ordinary man in extraordinary circumstances. That's why he, and all of their Stony Man colleagues, stood head and shoulders above the average citizen and lived damn larger than ordinary men.

And yet, it was the icy-eyed determination and grim but ruggedly handsome visage of Mack Bolan that always filled Price's mind when the chips were down. She never sat around and pined for the Executioner. When they could have time together, Price cherished it and treated it with unconditional respect.

Price smoothed her skirt and shook visions of Bolan from her mind. She turned her attention to the task at hand. At Brognola's request, she'd pulled everything the NSA had on reported activities for the New Islamic Front, everything from acts for which they claimed responsibility, to known sightings across the U.S. While Price would have preferred to work with Kurtzman on the information, she knew he was busy researching data for Able Team, who had started receiving and examining forensic evidence from the bombing. It was evidence Able Team had been glad to divert from its destination at the FBI laboratories in Fairfax, Virginia.

As Price began to sort through the information, collating enough data to prepare a brief for the Stony Man teams, she thought about what Bolan had gone up against in such a short period of time. First, there was the shoot-out in Arlington with Arab extremists carrying machine pistols, then the firebombing at DARPA headquarters. In both cases, it appeared Bolan was the target, but no one had a clue as to how or why. Even if he was identified as a new hire at the IPTO, what threat did he pose to the NIF? Unless they thought he was a replacement for Tyra MacEwan, in which case it seemed sensible to assume MacEwan's disappearance was somehow tied to the NIF. If members of the NIF were responsible for the murder of Dr. Fowler, it stood to reason that MacEwan—who'd been working very closely with him for many months—would drop out of sight. It had been seventy-two hours since her disappearance, and Price thought the chances of finding her were almost nil. Still, if anyone could locate her and bring her back alive, it was Bolan.

Price decided she'd let Bolan worry about MacEwan, and *she* would worry about feeding him information and watching his back.

As she studied the statistics, Price shook her head with dismay. It was estimated there were at least a thousand NIF members working and living inside the United States, and five hundred more suspected of membership or, at minimum, collusion. Some of those were Americans who swore a new allegiance to the Islamic world following the attacks on the Pentagon and World Trade Center.

Based on Internet traffic and interpretation of data from the SEC, some of those NIF members were CEOs and brokers for major corporations within the private and commercial sectors. There was also talk in the intelligence community that underground groups were arming themselves and preparing a major, coordinated strike against innocent American civilians.

Yet, no single piece of information seemed as important as the book of matches Bolan had found in the terrorist vehicle. Kurtzman had squeezed every bit of information—no matter how seemingly inconsequential—from his database on *Riyad Bari.* The Garden of Allah was a legitimate business whose owners paid taxes, and made significant contributions to worldwide organizations and consortiums of peace. The business was a perfect facade to mask horrible and violent activities.

The problem was that none of the federal law enforcement or security agencies had been able to find anything beyond coincidence, circumstantial evidence and vague conjecture that the Garden of Allah was anything more than it claimed: a multiethnic club that catered to rich Middle Easterners and Americans who'd sworn allegiance to the NIF.

It was going to take more than just good guesswork. Barbara Price would have to examine every bit of the information in the files, separate the wheat from the chaff and then get that information into the hands that would make the most use of it.

"Hi, Barb," Brognola said around an unlit cigar, stepping into her office in the Annex and taking a seat in front of her desk.

"Hello," Price replied. "I just got back, so I don't have a whole lot yet."

"I understand. Actually, I have something for you that might prove helpful in your research."

Price sat back in her chair. "I'm all ears. Shoot."

"Kissinger and Gadgets finished their initial inspection of the bomb parts recovered from DARPA. Gadgets says they got a lot of good pieces."

"Sounds like the federal boys have gotten better at evidence collection in the past few years."

"Yeah, and I don't wonder why," Brognola replied. "I don't think whoever blew that thing was worried about hiding their identity. Anyway, with Bear's help, they determined the other ingredient used in the bomb was C-4. We're guessing it's probably from a grade manufactured around the time of Desert Storm."

"Well, that seems to indicate Middle East terrorists," Price said.

"Yes, the black market for small arms and explosives was extremely active in Kuwait. However, it also makes it likely this is an organization operating independent of al Qaeda, and that bothers me because it essentially makes them much less predictable."

"You believe we really are dealing with the New Islamic Front?" Price asked.

Brognola nodded slowly with a grunt and a grim expression. "I don't think there's any doubt. Between what we're now hearing about Fowler's research, and given this new development with the Garden of Allah, I'm convinced that this could only be the work of the NIF."

"I was thinking that this almost fits too well, Hal."

The Stony Man chief cocked his head to one side as he pulled the cigar from his mouth. "Could you elaborate?"

"Well…I'm not sure yet, but it seems like this has been just a little too easy. If we *were* dealing with NIF terrorists who really did consider Striker a threat, they would have gone all out by now. They could just as easily have sent a small army as four men, but they didn't. They could have built a more powerful explosive and made sure they killed everyone in that office, yet they put it beneath a heavy, metal desk belonging to a secretary. It just doesn't make much sense."

"Well, we could interpret the hit on Striker in a number of ways, but I think you raise a good point as far as the bomb. You're thinking real terrorists who go to the risk of planting a bomb inside a federal defense agency would have been a bit more selective about their targets."

"Exactly. But the fact they didn't means they either weren't really interested in making a statement, or—"

"They did it to draw attention away from something else," Brognola said, finishing her thought.

Price nodded.

"You know, I think you're onto something," Brognola said after a pause. "I'm going to have Aaron start running checks on other activities around the city at the time the bomb went off. Maybe he can find something out of the ordinary."

The big Fed rose to leave, then on afterthought turned to look at Price. "I need you to follow up on another angle, Barb."

"Sure thing."

"If you're right, none of this explains the disappearance of MacEwan. We need to find out exactly what she and Fowler were working on. As soon as you're done compiling that info, start working the angles. When you have something solid, let me know and we'll find a way to pass the information to Striker."

Price nodded and Brognola turned and left.

It was well after midnight before members of the police and FBI released Bolan on his own recognizance. The Executioner considered himself lucky. He knew they could have detained him longer, had they so chosen. That would have meant having to make a call to Brognola, and he didn't want to draw that kind of attention if it was possible to avoid it.

After saying goodbye to Dr. Shurish, Bolan left the DARPA offices and decided to check into a different hotel than the one reserved for him. He picked a Motor Inn a few miles away from the original, one that provided easy highway access but was small and nondescript enough that he could be inconspicuous. That was especially important, looking the way he did, with a bandage on his forehead, reeking of expended gasoline and covered in soot.

Once he'd showered and changed, he decided to pay a visit to the Garden of Allah. Like most clubs in the area, the place probably stayed open until two or three a.m., so he still had time to do some looking around. His Beretta 93-R was tucked in shoulder leather beneath his left armpit; Bolan hoped he wouldn't need it.

He wanted a lead on the NIF, but he also wondered if he

would be able to get information on Fowler's murder or MacEwan's disappearance. Bolan still wasn't completely convinced the two incidents were connected. So the NIF would shoot Fowler in cold blood in the presence of dozens of witnesses, but then secretly move MacEwan to some unknown location? No, the Executioner couldn't buy that one. There was no logic to such a move, and it didn't fall into the modus operandi of most terrorist organizations. There had to be another explanation, and he was hell-bent on finding out what it was.

Bolan parked his car across the street from the club and studied the entrance. There were two large bruisers standing outside the door, admitting people. The soldier could see a third on the inside checking each entrant with a handheld metal detector. Well, so much for getting inside that way. Bolan didn't like the thought of going unarmed, especially since he was less than twelve hours into the mission and twice he'd been thrown directly into the line of fire. It was time to find another way inside.

Bolan got out of the car and followed the sidewalk to the end of the block. He crossed the street and walked to an alleyway entrance he'd first spotted while driving into the area. The alley ran between the establishments on the same block as the club, and those on the next one over. This was one of the nicer parts of the city, and the alley provided a route for deliveries and trash pickup that wouldn't clutter the streets.

Bolan hopped a metal-and-plastic-meshwork fence that bordered the back of the club. He found the rear door and studied it. It was made from heavy wood with metal reinforcement, and was probably bolted from the inside. The Executioner frowned, and then an idea came to him. A sign pointed to a bell for deliveries, and the Executioner stabbed the button to sound it. A few moments passed before a guy opened a slide in the door.

"Yeah?" he asked in heavily accented English.

The guy could barely see over the top of the door, but Bolan could see he was young. The Executioner immediately went into role camouflage, flashing the guy an expression that said he was cold, tired and not in a great mood.

He jerked his thumb over his shoulder and grunted, "I got booze."

"We have enough already," the kid replied.

"Special delivery," Bolan said, pretending to look down to a clipboard. "Somebody named Ibn...something or other. I can't read half these damn names they give me. Our dispatcher and her chicken scratch, you know?"

"Well, leave it at the door," the kid said.

Bolan scratched the back of his head. "I can do that, I guess, but just don't tell my boss. And you still gotta sign. How 'bout you take this and sign it while I go get the stuff."

"All right," the kid said, shutting the slider.

Bolan quickly moved to the side of the door and waited to spring. There was the sound of a bolt sliding, then another, and Bolan watched as the silvery door handle began to turn. He tensed slightly as the door opened, then reached around and grabbed a handful of shirt. The soldier hauled the kid through the partially open door, pushed him up against the wall and landed a rock-hard punch behind his ear. He caught the kid's body as it slumped to the ground, and dragged him over to the area behind some garbage bins.

Once inside, Bolan secured the door and quickly took in his surroundings. It was a small room with a table and chair positioned in one corner beneath a bare lightbulb dangling from the ceiling. A cigarette smoldered in an ashtray next to half-full bottle of whiskey and a deck of cards. Obviously, the kid was supposed to just sit around and wait for something, but just what that something was remained a mystery.

Bolan immediately moved over to the table and shut off the overhead light. He could hear the music booming in the club area, the bass sounds thumping and reverberating against the walls. It didn't sound like Middle Eastern music. From appearances alone, the Garden of Allah was a typical American dance club.

He waited a couple of minutes for his eyes to adjust, then went to the interior door and opened it. A long hallway stretched out in either direction. Bolan checked both ways, insured the hallway was empty, then stepped out of the sparse back room and closed the door behind him. There was another door immediately across the hall.

Bolan tried the handle and it was locked. He thought a minute about kicking it in, but that would only attract attention, and there was no evidence anything on the other side would aid him in his quest. Bolan decided to bide his time and join the party. He was bound to catch a break eventually, after all, and he didn't want to do anything that might compromise his already precarious position.

He walked down the hallway in the direction of the music and pushed his way through another door. His senses were immediately assaulted with the sounds and smells of dancing people, tobacco smoke and rock music. He could hear it was a modernization of traditional Arabic music; traditional instruments contrasted with electric guitars and drums in a throbbing beat.

The Executioner quickly closed the door behind him. He was near the dance floor in a pretty inconspicuous area, and he noticed that the door actually blended with the rest of the wall. It was probably meant to serve as an unmarked service entrance to the back. Bolan studied his surroundings, and it didn't appear that anybody who worked in the club even took notice of him. They were too busy catering to the hundreds of patrons.

The place itself was decorated like an Arabian palace. Scarlet roll pillows and shin-high tables were scattered throughout the room. There were rugs on the walls and floors, and the very traditional décor was spread throughout several levels—almost like graduated tiers—that all bordered the dance floor. Bolan moved around the edge of dance area, which was cluttered with people doing an assortment of bump-and-grind dance moves. There were two circular podiums anchored in the middle of the dance floor, and a pair of dark-haired, dark-eyed beauties in skimpy outfits were writhing and twisting in various intriguing directions not necessarily in rhythm with the music.

Bolan continued through the club, looking for a place to sit that would provide him with an unobstructed view. He decided on the bar when he couldn't find anything in the crowded dance area. The warrior ordered tonic water with lime, and waited. He had barely taken a sip from his drink when a beautiful young woman slinked onto the stool next to him, making an effort to brush his arm.

"Excuse me," she said politely.

Bolan nodded but found it hard to take his eyes from her. She had cocoa-colored skin and dark, inquisitive eyes. Her black curly hair seemed to explode from her head and dance down her back, remnants spilling onto her lean shoulders. She was dressed in a red, strapless dress that rode up her thighs when she crossed her shapely legs. Yeah, definitely hot—and *definitely* trouble.

"My name is Fadilah. What's yours?" she asked, smiling.

"Matt," Bolan replied. He didn't like this at all. The woman was very attractive, and that meant she would draw attention—something he couldn't afford. "Hey, I'm sorry but I have to run," he said, apologetically.

"Why?" Her eyes flashed in the brilliant changes in the lights corresponding with a change in the music. "Don't you like me?"

"Yeah, I like you," Bolan replied. "It's just—"

"Then stay and talk with me." She patted the bar. It took Bolan only a second to notice that as she'd drawn his attention by patting the bar, she'd also drawn a P-93 pistol, although he could only guess where she'd been hiding it. She smiled and added, "Please?"

Bolan looked at her a moment and then a movement caught his attention. He noticed it only because it was a forceful and purposeful movement, and it was coming in his direction. It was still kind of dark, but Bolan immediately recognized one of the two men approaching. It was the driver he had shot earlier that day.

The Executioner looked into the woman's eyes. "I think you've made a mistake."

"No, Matt, I think it is you who have made the mistake," she said.

Bolan shook his head. "Think again."

The Executioner stepped back suddenly and tossed his drink in the woman's face. Her reaction was immediate and expected, and while it was a risky move, it was enough of a diversion for Bolan to act.

The medical people call it diver's reflex. When the face is suddenly splashed with ice-cold water, it stimulates the vagus nerve, which is partially responsible for motor and sensory stimulation of the stomach, heart and lungs. As Fadilah sucked in a deep breath, her body relaxed enough for Bolan to arrest her arm, snatch the gun from her hand and spin her on the bar stool. The Executioner then wrapped a muscular arm around her throat as he pointed her pistol in the direction of the approaching men.

As people around him began to scream and react to the situation, Bolan continued concentrating on his enemy. And as the two men moved for cover and drew weapons of their own, the Executioner squeezed the trigger.

Smallwood State Park, Maryland

TYRA MACEWAN WIPED the tears of exhaustion from her eyes and leaned back from the screen of her laptop computer. The creaminess of melting marshmallows tickled her upper lip as she sipped hot cocoa from a mug. The cocoa felt warm and sweet going down, and it boosted her spirits a little. She was tired from staying awake for more than forty-eight hours straight, trying every trick she knew to find out what was going on. She stared at the fireplace, listening to the wood crackle and pop, willing herself not to become mesmerized by the effects of shadows—cast by the flickering orange flames—dancing on the walls.

The work was mind numbing, but she knew she couldn't give up. The security of the entire country was at stake; she was certain of that much. She'd made that discovery pretty early on when she hacked into the FBI systems and began to review all of Fowler's notes and files. His research had been extensive, no question of that, and it was only his personal electronic journal that had helped point her in the right direction—given her something for which to look.

MacEwan was relieved she'd immediately backed up all of his files to a set of three micro CD-ROMs, because shortly after she hacked into the systems, she discovered the FBI had cleared everything from Fowler's system and moved it God only knew where. That was okay, though, because it would take them some time to hack through security codes and passwords that she already knew.

MacEwan and Fowler had become fast friends over the short time they worked together. Five months. Five months was all she got to spend with him, but she'd grown to like him very much, and more importantly she'd respected him. It was difficult for anyone to earn her respect easily. MacEwan realized Fowler was so very much like her that it was only natural she'd come to enjoy his company. He'd had a brilliant mind and keen intuition for technological advancements that were so unusual and astute that she surmised he was years ahead of his colleagues. But most important was that he'd had an insatiable curiosity and love for anything technical, and MacEwan shared his passions. Through it all, they had kept things purely professional.

It wasn't that MacEwan didn't consider him a choice candidate. He would have been a decent catch, and she was certain her mom would have liked him. But he never made an advance; he just treated her with the respect of a kindred scientist and an intellectual equal. She would desperately miss him, and she knew that the best way to pay homage to his memory would be to find those responsible for his death. She knew she was getting close when she got her first break.

She didn't have any hard evidence yet, but her discoveries

had led her to conclude that someone was showing more than a passing interest in the FBI's packet sniffing software, known publicly as the Carnivore system. There had always been risks associated with Carnivore, not only in the unauthorized acquisition of electronic communication information belonging to private and publicly traded corporations, but also to other government agencies. It was beginning to look like someone else had attempted, or was attempting to exploit those risks. MacEwan was certain it was that discovery that had led to Fowler's murder, and it would lead to the same conclusion for her if she wasn't careful.

She didn't have the first clue who. Of course, her first theory—and the least likely—was that the penetration of Carnivore had simply been inadvertent, that some computer geek had found a hole in the system and hacked through it. MacEwan quickly dismissed the idea because the same lack of evidence that prevented her or the FBI from identifying the hackers also supported the theory this was a deliberate act.

An alternate theory pointed toward cybercriminals. Perhaps the Mafia or some other organized crime element bent on using Carnivore to steal money, or possibly even lives. That kind of thinking fit a variety of angles, especially since using technology, particularly the Internet, for identity theft had become very popular in the past few years. By parsing and rearranging the bits and bytes of data stored on nearly any individual in America, criminals could forge social security numbers, high school and college transcripts, driver's licenses and just about anything else they wished. With the push of a button, cybercriminals could assign virtual identities with complete personal histories to ex-cons or fugitives—and they could also use these abilities in the same fashion to blackmail victims or destroy the lives of their enemies.

Then there was the most frightening thought of all: terrorists. For years, intelligence reports had been flooding various U.S. agencies urging government officials to put in place better security controls on electronic information. It just seemed like many weren't aware of the potential threat. From her first real interest in computers to her graduation from MIT, MacEwan had always known she wanted to specialize in the area of increased security for America's information highways. She'd been in school and watched as terrorists seized control of planes. She could remember sitting in her college dorm room on that fateful September morning, eyes glued to the television set, watching with horror as the World Trade Center towers collapsed and the Pentagon burned with unchecked fury.

It was then that she knew her dream to become an information security expert for the American government was her passion—her calling. MacEwan's graduation from MIT and subsequent assignment to DARPA proved the vehicle by which her dreams became fully realized. What she hadn't counted on was her job bringing her into such mortal danger—that was her own, stupid naiveté. Somebody had killed Fowler, and they wouldn't hesitate to kill her next if they found out where she was hiding, and what she was doing.

MacEwan shook herself back to the present and studied more of the Carnivore schematics. It was actually a brilliantly designed program, probably the crown jewel of information retrieval systems. It was capable of "sniffing" through all layers of an information gateway, on intranets or extranets, checking and analyzing each individual packet of information and looking for key elements: a catchword, a nonsensible code, a phrase. There were certain words that would set off warning alarms, and certain communications between specific areas that required special attention—most important were international communications, whether e-mails, financial transactions, instant messages, or the like.

Carnivore was also intended to monitor all government communications. In general, employees were not authorized to use government information systems for personal communication, so anyone caught doing so was usually subject to disciplinary action. Nonetheless, people were going to be people, and most of the time they weren't going to listen and follow the rules. Thus, they took the risks that their personal communications were immediately subject to inspection. It had always been a hotbed of legal activity where Carnivore was concerned. MacEwan hadn't ruled out the possibility that this was a deliberate act meant to "expose" Carnivore to the public eye, especially to the scrutiny of the press and Congress.

Still, everyone knew it was there and what it was capable of, and as long as the government didn't abuse it the American people would accept it. The minute someone stepped over the line that would be another story entirely. So if this were the work of cyberterrorists, not only could hacking into the system create a threat to information systems around the country, but also wreak havoc with the democratic infrastructure of the American political machine.

The concept of creating severe inner turmoil to destroy a country wasn't a new one, and it certainly wasn't above the methodologies of terrorist organizations around the world. If their sole purpose was to destroy American freedoms, they would go to any lengths to achieve those ends.

MacEwan was going to have to go through the system directly in order to find out what was really going on. Then and only then would she be able to figure out how to shut it down. She knew the hackers might be able to detect her presence in the system, but she had to risk it. She owed that much to Mitch Fowler. She would do her duty, even if it meant she might be on the run for the rest of her life. But MacEwan was enough of a realist to know she couldn't evade them forever.

And when they finally did come for her, she knew there wouldn't be a knight in shining armor ready to defend her to the death.

4

Washington, D.C.

Fadilah screamed and cursed in protest as Bolan kept his enemy behind cover with a steady barrage of 9 mm rounds. The woman tried to twist out of the Executioner's viselike grip while being dragged backward to the far end of the bar, which was the best cover at that point.

Bolan uttered a sharp word for her to settle down, gripping the thick silk of her dress tighter as he continued retreating, ever careful to keep the woman between him and the enemy. The slide on the Polish-made pistol locked back as Bolan reached the end of the bar. He pushed the woman to the floor behind the bar and pinned her there with his foot on the small of her back as he drew his Beretta.

He wondered for just a second how he'd gotten himself into this mess. He hadn't even had time to really assess the situation before the enemy latched on to him for the third time in one day. Something was definitely rotten, and Bolan needed to figure out how they kept popping up everywhere he did.

Not that it mattered at that moment—his time was better spent making sure he didn't wind up on a slab in the local morgue. Bolan gripped the weapon, careful to keep it out of sight as he thumbed the selector. The two attackers had exposed themselves, obviously convinced he was no longer a threat, since they had seen Fadilah's pistol run dry. Bolan knew he had a distinct advantage if the pair of killers approaching with a vengeance acted as predictably as he expected.

They did.

Bolan waited until they were close enough for him to take both quickly, but not in such a position they could find cover. He produced the Beretta from behind the bar and first took his nemesis from the morning attack with a double-tap. This time, the guy wasn't lucky enough to escape alive from an encounter with the Executioner as both rounds struck him in the chest. One of the subsonic rounds ripped through lung and muscle tissue, while the other exploded his heart. The guy vomited blood as the impact threw him against the bar and then knocked him facedown to the ground.

Bolan fired at the other target who was now frozen in place with a horrified expression. The 9 mm slug wiped that expression from his face as it punched through his upper lip and continued out the back of his head. People were screaming, but they had cleared out of the immediate area of fire, so Bolan was less concerned about innocents getting hit.

He waited a moment or two to make sure his opponents didn't move, then hauled Fadilah to her feet and shoved her in the direction of the door set in the wall. She walked ahead of him stiffly, and Bolan noticed she seemed unconcerned they were walking toward a seemingly blank wall. That meant she was familiar with the layout of the club, which also meant she was most likely associated in some way with the New Islamic Front.

"Open it," Bolan said when they reached the door. She turned slightly and looked at him, trying to act puzzled, but Bolan wasn't falling for it. "You heard me. I know it's there, so stop wasting time."

The club was empty, and Bolan could hear the pounding of boots approaching from behind. He turned in time to see three men enter the room, all toting M-85 submachine guns. They immediately spotted Bolan and Fadilah and opened fire. Bullets peppered the area around them, shattering the ashtrays on nearby tables and ripping deep gashes in the carpeted walls.

Bolan capped off several quick shots from the Beretta as he pushed Fadilah through the opening. He slammed the door closed once they were on the other side and directed her down the hallway with a wave of the Beretta. She fired him a hateful look before complying. Bolan knew she would eventually make a break for it, but it wasn't time for that yet. He grabbed her by the arm when they reached the locked door he'd discovered when he'd first gained entrance to the club.

"Stop. What's behind this door?" he asked.

"I do not know," she replied quickly.

"Sorry, wrong answer." Bolan pushed her to one side and put his foot to the door. The wall shook with the force, but surprisingly—even under the power of the Executioner's strength—the door wouldn't budge.

"Reinforced," Bolan said, eyeing the woman. "No reason to reinforce a door if you don't have something to hide."

Nonetheless, the Executioner knew they were running out of time, and he couldn't waste it working on the locked door. He would have to wait for another opportunity to come back and figure out what they were hiding at the Garden of Allah.

Bolan pushed open the door to the back room, and fired a

few more rounds at the trio of gunmen entering the hallway. As he pushed Fadilah into the room, he wondered how easy it would be to get away from their pursuers. They had undoubtedly followed him here, which meant they might be watching his vehicle. Worse yet, they might even have booby-trapped it, but it was his fastest way out of there with his prisoner intact.

The Executioner nodded as an idea suddenly came to him. Instead of going through the back door, he simply opened it, then pushed Fadilah to the darkened corner of the room. He quickly upended the table for cover, then pushed her down behind it and lay on top of her. As the door from the hallway opened, Bolan clamped his hand around the woman's mouth and squeezed her windpipe and carotid arteries between thumb and forefinger. It was enough to keep her quiet as the gunmen rushed right past them and out the open door.

Bolan jumped to his feet after counting to thirty and quietly closed the back door, bolting it from the inside and effectively locking out the enemy troops. That would buy them enough time to get to his sedan. He went back to the table and retrieved his prisoner, who was still woozy from a brain starved of oxygenated blood.

The Executioner found it difficult to feel sorry for her. He knew this woman would castrate him and slit his throat, given half the chance. She was a terrorist—or at least in league with terrorists. Bolan had no doubts. Frankly, he couldn't have cared less. Duty and integrity drove the Executioner's actions where enemy prisoners were considered, and he would follow the humane rules of warfare unless Fadilah gave him a reason to do otherwise.

They reached the car unmolested, and Bolan unlocked the

driver's side door and shoved the woman into the front seat. He climbed behind the wheel, reached beneath the seat and withdrew a pair of plastic riot cuffs, then holstered the Beretta.

"Put your hands behind your head," he ordered.

At first, she didn't look like she was going to comply, then she did as she was told with a cold precision that left no doubt in Bolan's mind he was dealing with a cold and calculating killer. He'd seen that look in the eyes of the enemy before: the bloodthirsty gaze of vengeance and hatred that seemed to come along with any fanaticism. It was the look of a murderous extremist, and he could imagine she was probably cursing him in her mind. Yet she kept it totally professional, maintaining a stoic, impassive expression as Bolan cuffed her hands to the metal sliders of the headrest.

Her body looked seductive in that position, the skirt revealing a considerable amount of thigh while her hands were effectively tied behind her head. The full, voluptuous breasts pushed against the silky material, which shimmered in the streetlights. The look in Fadilah's eyes changed as she realized how exposed she was, and the expression told Bolan she thought no ordinary man would be able to resist succumbing to such fleshly pleasures.

But she didn't know Mack Bolan.

The Executioner didn't even give her an appreciative look before putting the luxury car in gear and getting away from there as quickly as he could. He got a few miles from the club, heading to a nearby abandoned pier that overlooked the Potomac. Under other circumstances it would have been a romantic site, but Bolan recognized the odd twist that it was also the best place for an interrogation.

Bolan turned to the woman. "You work for the NIF." It was a statement rather than a question.

"I do not know who you mean," she said, feigning innocence.

Bolan withdrew the Beretta and aimed it at her feet. "You think I won't start one toe at a time?"

"You will not," she replied with a defiant shake of her head. "I have seen you in action. You are not that kind of man."

Bolan's face went hard, and he looked directly in her eyes. The twin pools of blue bored right through her, and something in his gut—something seemingly forged from a mix of anger and adrenaline—pushed a lump to his throat. Yeah, she was right; he wouldn't have done it. But there was something in her face that he figured had her reconsidering her position.

Bolan decided to play on that as he cocked the hammer and said, "I'm sorry you think that."

The Executioner squeezed the trigger, and the sound of the shot was deafening inside the car. The woman jumped in her seat, obviously intimidated and obviously paying full attention to her captor.

"Damn…I missed. Well, I never miss twice, so let's try again. Are you with the New Islamic Front?" Bolan asked.

"Y-yes," she managed through clenched teeth. She was now squirming in the seat, trying to get free of her bonds, but to no avail. She didn't possess the strength to snap the thick plastic cuffs or break the headrest. Most men didn't have that kind of strength, so Bolan didn't find any reason to be worried. For the moment, she was truly a captive audience.

"Whatever you are planning to do to me, I beg you to kill me when you are finished," she said.

Bolan was surprised by her comment. "What are you talking about?"

"I am still a virgin. No man has had me, and no man will until it is my husband. I know you will get what you need, and then you will take my body. From one warrior to another, I ask you to kill me when you are done. A woman who loses her virginity to any man other than her husband is shamed."

"Lady, I'm not a murderer or a rapist," Bolan replied. "Now, cut the drama and tell me what you've done with Tyra MacEwan."

"I have done nothing with her."

"Then where's she being held?"

"I do not know. We have not found her yet. My brothers are looking for her. When they find her they will kill her."

Before Bolan could ask another question, his cell phone began to ring.

"Yeah?" Bolan said, answering the phone without taking his eyes off his informant.

"Striker, this is Bear. I think maybe we've found MacEwan."

"Where?"

"A place called Smallwood State Park. She rented a cabin down there for a month under an alias of Marsha Graham. I caught her trying to hack into one of the systems I've been monitoring. She was using quite a few good back doors, and I almost didn't catch it. As it is, it took me a while to get the information."

"I know right where it's at. I'll head there now."

"Understood. You may want to call me back in ten so I can give you a more accurate location."

"Check. Out here." Bolan disconnected the call and looked at his prisoner with a frosty glare. "Lady, this is your lucky night. Out." He yanked a pocketknife from his jacket and cut her bonds.

"It is freezing out there," she said.

Bolan made a show of pulling everything from his jacket pockets, then shed the coat and handed it to her with a hard stare. "You can stay and take your chances with me if you want."

She tossed the coat around her shoulders, opened the door and bailed. As soon as she'd shut the door, Bolan left her standing in the abandoned parking lot with a squeal of tires. He watched her stand there, her shivering form rapidly disappearing in the rearview mirror. She would most likely find a phone and call her people, give them some story about how she'd outwitted him, managed to take him off guard and escape, or that she'd convinced him she wasn't involved with the NIF. The thought of it pleased Bolan.

Yeah, that was exactly what the Executioner was counting on.

It took Bolan an hour to reach Smallwood State Park. The place was essentially deserted. The registrar, of course, remembered Ms. Graham because she was one of the few guests in the entire park. Very rarely did someone reserve a cabin at this time of year, especially not one beside Mattawoman Creek, which was completely frozen over. Of course, she was glad to meet Mr. Cooper, Ms. Graham's brother, but apologetic there was no phone in the cabin, so he couldn't call ahead from the office to let her know he was coming up. Bolan thanked the woman for her help and handed her a twenty-dollar bill in apology for the early hour.

Bolan parked his car in an area clear of snow and mud. He went EVA and rather than heading up the main trail, decided to follow the route on the map from the wood line.

The whole situation had left Bolan feeling edgy. Kurtzman was nothing short of a genius in the technology field, and the warrior would have been the first to admit it. But if he was able to find MacEwan so quickly, that meant the enemy might find her just as easily. This was especially true given the fact that Fadilah hadn't even blinked when Bolan mentioned MacEwan's name. That confirmed some link between Mac-Ewan and the NIF, which also made it likely that the NIF was behind Fowler's death.

The only thing that didn't connect was why. Bolan could only hope that MacEwan would be able to contribute that piece of the puzzle. By then, Fadilah would have made contact with her people, and Bolan would have enough intelligence to take the offensive. Frankly, he was tired of being the punching bag. It was time to give back.

Bolan counted the cabins as he passed them. It seemed like it was going to take him forever, and he was beginning to wonder if this had been such a good idea, but he decided to keep going rather than forsaking his first plan and returning for his vehicle. It was nearly forty-five minutes before he reached number 16, and in the light of first dawn, he could make out footprints in the snow. They were fresh, and too large to be MacEwan's—not to mention the fact there were two separate pairs.

Bolan checked the action on the Beretta; he'd already reloaded a fresh clip. He reached beneath his jacket to the small of his back and retrieved the Desert Eagle. He checked its action as well as he entered the woods and scrambled quietly but quickly through the brush and brambles until he had a clear view of the back entrance to MacEwan's cabin.

Bolan didn't hear anything, didn't detect any movement, but he could see the light spilling through points around the drawn curtains. All of them were drawn. Bolan's sixth sense immediately went into overdrive. Something was wrong with the whole scene. First, it was strange that MacEwan would welcome visitors at such an early hour. But more importantly, it was quiet—as quiet as death.

Bolan waited another minute or two before deciding to proceed to the back door, which was only ten or twelve yards beyond the wood line. As Bolan drew closer, he kept the Desert Eagle ahead of him in a Weaver's grip, tracking at forty-five to ninety degrees, covering all angles when appropriate. The last thing he needed was to be taken by sentries. Still, he'd only seen two sets of tracks. That meant either park staff or enemy. Bolan was betting on the latter. He knew he was right when he pressed his ear to the door and heard whimpering and a snapping sound. It was the sound a belt made on flesh.

The old wooden door was no match for Bolan's six-foot-three, two-hundred-pound frame as he kicked it off its hinges. Neither were the two surprised terrorists any match for the Desert Eagle now booming and kicking in Bolan's grip. His first round took the closer terrorist in the head, splitting his skull apart and spraying his partner with bloody flesh and gray matter.

The second terrorist seemed more concerned about trying to bring his pistol to bear with the intent of shooting the nude woman tied to the chair than he did about defending himself. That was his fatal mistake as Bolan took him with two .44 Magnum slugs in the chest. The terrorist's body slammed against a nearby wall with enough force to split open the back of his head. His corpse collapsed to the wooden floor, leaving a cloud of dust to rise in the wake.

The woman stared at Bolan with wide-eyed fear.

"It's okay," Bolan said gently. He lowered the pistol and

raised his free hand to show he wasn't going to hurt her. "I'm here to help you."

Bolan approached her slowly, not wanting to brutalize her emotions anymore than her now dead captors already had. She was tied to an overstuffed chair, her legs secured at the ankles, and there were significant raised welts on both of her thighs. She was also bleeding from her nose, and there was a bruise rapidly forming under her left cheekbone.

Bolan quickly cut her bonds, went to the bedroom and returned a moment later with a blanket, then started for the kitchen. "We need to get some ice on those welts."

"W-wait p-please," MacEwan stammered, raising her hand and trying to shake her head free of the fog. "Who are you?"

"One of the good guys," Bolan replied.

5

After inspection with a practiced eye, the Executioner determined Tyra MacEwan's wounds weren't serious.

The IT expert looked at him searchingly. Bolan had to admit, she was some looker: early-thirties, full dark curly hair, a natural pout to her full red lips and brown eyes that seemed almost iridescent in the cabin's lighting. The woman's body had no less its own qualities, and Bolan couldn't help noticing the firm curves and lines that betrayed the fact she probably spent time three to four days a week at the gym.

"Do you want a doctor?" Bolan asked her.

"Do I need one?" she asked in return.

The soldier shrugged and tried to smile with reassurance. "The ice will help with the welts. I don't think you have any broken bones, and I don't see any open wounds."

MacEwan shivered visibly inside the blanket as she replied, "They took their time."

"Were you sexually assaulted?"

Bolan could see by her expression and the way she suddenly looked up from the steaming cup of tea that the question stung a bit; he hadn't meant it to but he needed to be sure. MacEwan just shook her head in way of reply, then dropped her gaze to the cup again.

"Good." Bolan rose from the couch and went to the bodies. He was hoping the park was deserted enough that no one heard the reports from the shooting. While MacEwan sat in the chair, wrapped in a blanket and icing her legs, Bolan searched the bodies for identification. He was surprised to find driver's licenses identifying the men as Abbas Ben Kalil and Yasin Muhamduh. There was no other identification, such as legal immigrant cards, which most likely meant that either these IDs were fakes or the men were U.S. citizens. If it were the latter, it was only more reason for concern in Bolan's mind.

"Do you know either of these men?" Bolan asked MacEwan.

"No. I've never seen them before in my life."

Bolan nodded as he came back to the couch and sat. He stared intently at her, but she met his gaze. There was no challenge or fear in her eyes, but rather a strange sort of inquisitiveness. She was obviously just as curious about her rescuer as Bolan was about her.

"Tell me something, Tyra. Why did you take off? What are you running from?"

She appeared surprised as she replied, "You know my name. You have me at a disadvantage, since I don't know your name, and I'm guessing you probably know everything about me."

"Just about," Bolan admitted. "You can call me Cooper…or Matt, if you prefer. And you still haven't answered my questions."

MacEwan sighed deeply, then said, "I'm not even sure what I'm running from, Matt, or *who* for that matter. What I can tell you is that I was assigned to work with the FBI's technology people on the Carnivore system. You're familiar with that?"

"A little. I was given a short briefing before being assigned to the IPTO as your replacement."

"Replacement? You're a technologist of some kind then."

"A scientist. Like you."

She lifted one eyebrow and said, "Why do I find that hard to believe?"

"You were saying that you were assigned to work on Carnivore. Tell me more about that."

"You have top security clearance?"

Bolan nodded.

"All right, I guess it can't hurt me at this point. The Carnivore system is essentially classified to the general public as an Internet packet sniffer. But I'm guessing you probably know it's a lot more than that."

Bolan smiled. "I understand the basic concepts of Carnivore. I'm more familiar with the controversy surrounding its invasion of private and confidential data."

"That's been at the center of arguments both for and against such a tool in the hands of government officials and law-enforcement agencies. Not only have other state and federal institutions expressed concerns, but also private organizations and the general public...and with good reason."

"You think Carnivore poses a threat to the American people?" Bolan asked.

"Anything that has the ability to monitor e-mail transmissions, data transfers, and database searching capabilities could be a tremendous threat if it fell into the wrong hands. And that's what I and my FBI liaison discovered might be happening. We just didn't have time to prove it before he died."

"You're talking about Fowler?"

MacEwan looked at him a moment before whispering, "Yes."

"I'm sorry about that. Were you close?" Bolan continued his questioning.

"I considered him a friend, and respected him as a scientist. He had an unusual mind for this field, and was more brilliant in the areas of technology than anyone I've ever known. I'd first heard about him at MIT. He'd attended before me. Some of his papers and theories were required reading, and I'd even heard him lecture on campus a few times. I considered it a privilege when I found out he'd selected me to work with him on Carnivore."

"What led you and Fowler to conclude someone compromised Carnivore's security system?"

"That's where it gets a bit more complicated. I hadn't seen an update on Mitchell's files until I hacked into the system. I'm assuming that's how you found me?"

Bolan jerked a thumb over his shoulder. "It's how they found you, too. That probably wasn't your brightest move. You should have gone for help."

"Gone to who?" she asked, her face flushing. "Mitch called me late the night before he was shot. He was hysterical. He kept…kept rambling on about how he thought someone had hacked inside the system, but he was still running tests, and he thought maybe it was terrorists or possibly organized crime elements. I've never seen him so shaken up." Tears began welling in her eyes as she continued, "And then before I could meet him, he's gunned down in front of a hundred witnesses. How was I supposed to know I wouldn't be next? What would you have done?"

"Just calm down," Bolan said in a hushed tone, raising his hand. "Relax. You're safe now. I probably would have done the same thing. But there are a lot of people out there right now concerned with your safety. It's my job to keep you alive."

"I thought you were just a scientist hired to replace me?" She looked concerned.

"For now, that's my story and I'm sticking to it. Please don't push me on that," Bolan said.

MacEwan didn't reply immediately; instead, she studied the big guy for some time.

Bolan could almost see the wheels of that intelligent mind turning as she thought through all of the moves. In many ways, she reminded him of Barbara Price, but she was entirely different in others. She certainly didn't have Barb's emotional maturity. No, this one was definitely more prone to outbursts and sudden mood swings. Some experts considered that a sign of creativity and high intelligence, so it didn't really bother Bolan. He'd definitely have to keep an eye on her, though, because people with personalities like MacEwan's had a tendency to make sudden and rash decisions when they felt out of control. He wasn't sure MacEwan could keep a level head in the custody of federal agents. He'd have to keep her close to him for a while, build her trust and confidence.

"So you hacked into Fowler's files." Bolan prodded her to continue.

"Yes," she said, visibly calmer now as she wiped away the tears falling freely down her reddened cheeks.

"And what did you find?"

"Can you bring that laptop to me?" she asked.

Bolan rose and went to the small wooden table adjacent to the kitchen. He returned with her portable computer and set it on the ottoman in front of her.

She put down the teacup and once signed into her system, began to peck rapidly at the keyboard.

"What are you doing?" Bolan asked.

"Running what's called a command line scripting file," she said. "It was something Mitch and I developed together and memorized, so that if something ever happened to either of us, we could just do the very thing we're doing now."

"Scripting file," Bolan repeated thoughtfully. "Is that some sort of security program?"

"In a sense. It allows us to embed objects and hide them within a system, so that if someone were to hack into our computer, they wouldn't actually see those objects, and thus wouldn't know they were there. In order for the objects to become visible, they must be able to run the proper scripts."

"What do you mean by objects?"

MacEwan stopped typing and looked at him with a half smile. "Scientist, huh? Now I know why I didn't believe you before." She returned to her work and continued her explanation. "In most cases, an object is simply a target file that contains two things—data and code. I think I managed to get all of the data from Mitchell's files downloaded. Now all I need to do is rerun the script."

She finished with an exaggerated press of the Enter key and after a few beeps from the system, she smiled with satisfaction. She leaned forward, squinting a moment at the screen, then turned the laptop so that Bolan could view the screen as well.

"Here are the files he didn't want anyone but me to find. Before the script, they wouldn't have been visible, even to most hacking tools and known script cracking programs. We use our own proprietary language and a special compiler to build that language. So even if someone could figure out the script, they still wouldn't be able to build or run it without the compiler installed on their system as well."

"Interesting," Bolan said. "And pretty complicated."

MacEwan winked at him before returning her attention to the screen, saying, "That's why they pay us the big bucks, Matt."

She was about to say more when something on the screen caught her attention. She looked at it more closely and then wrinkled her nose. Something had her puzzled, and Bolan was about to ask her what it was, but then thought better of it. He needed to just let her work, and she'd tell him what she thought he had to know. It was just a matter of time.

After close scrutiny, MacEwan invoked a text editor and began to type more information at a blinding pace. Most of what she typed into the editor looked like gibberish to the soldier, but it obviously made perfect sense to MacEwan. Every so often, the technical genius would stop and think, then input additional information. Eventually, she finished and entered the information, dragged some files into the viewer using the touchpad on the laptop, and then a viewer displayed on the LCD-panel.

. She pointed to a series of red and green lines, and a flashing red signal. "There! You see it?"

"Yeah. What does it mean?" Bolan asked.

"It means that's how whoever is doing this got in!" MacEwan explained.

"So someone has definitely cracked the Carnivore system."

"Oh, they've done more than cracked it. I'd be willing to bet that they're slowly and quietly taking control of it. In fact, they may already have control," she said.

"Can you find out who?"

"I'm not sure I can find out who, Matt, but with some time I can certainly find out *where*." She finished her statement with a cluck of her tongue.

"You mean trace the signal back to its source?"

"Yes."

"Good enough. Then maybe I can help you on that note." Bolan excused himself and went to the bedroom. He dialed the secure number and directly accessed the Farm. Barbara Price answered immediately.

"It's Striker."

"How are you?"

Bolan could hear the sincere concern in her voice. "I'm good. I found our little friend just in time. She was about to become raw meat for our terrorist friends."

"NIF?" Price asked.

"Probably. I'm sure you already heard about the trouble at the Garden of Allah?"

"Yes, we've been seeing the reports coming in all night."

"I managed to pull one of them out of there. As soon as I get this one settled in, I'm going to follow up on that."

"How did you arrange that?" Price asked.

Although he knew she couldn't see him, Bolan smiled into the phone as he replied, "I just did the gentlemanly thing and gave a lady my coat."

Washington, D.C.

SADIQ RHATIB SAT BACK in his chair, smiled and rubbed his hands together with glee. He'd found the American bitch who tried to outwit him during her attempts to hack into the FBI's security systems.

He'd turned the very program the egotistical Americans had used to spy on Rhatib's people, as well as their own, against them. Within a few weeks, perhaps sooner, he would be in complete control of every element in the Carnivore system, and would use it against anyone his master desired.

In reality, Rhatib cared little for his master's plans. He had a far more tangible idea for the use of Carnivore. Once he had control and had made the necessary modifications, Rhatib would be able to use Carnivore to control American defense systems in his country. This would include *all* of the systems, from satellite communications to offensive missile control of American ships and aircraft. He would then turn those weapons against the savages who oppressed his people. This would prove instrumental in restoring control of Afghanistan to his Taliban brothers.

Rhatib could hardly contain the anger that burned inside him. From very early in his life, he'd shown significant promise and knowledge in the areas of technology, particularly computer communications. Using monies and facilities supported by the al Qaeda network, Rhatib was sent to a secret training facility in Pakistan at the tender age of twelve. By the time he'd reached his sixteenth birthday, he'd proved and tested with an intelligence and core knowledge well exceeding that of some of the most brilliant and educated minds in the world.

Then the Americans lashed out in anger against Afghanistan, attacking without warning, destroying everything in their path and killing anything that got in their way. The American invasion had been nothing more than a vicious and unprovoked assault on a sovereign country, fueled by the desire for unholy vengeance and in support of a group of dissidents in the north who called themselves "freedom fighters." But where had those so-called freedom fighters been when the Soviet military came crashing through the country? Where were they when poorly armed and untrained mujahideen warriors defended their women and children—in fact their very existence—against the Russian invaders? The fact was, they weren't there and they didn't assist, and it was only by the perfect will of Allah that they survived and pushed the Soviet military machine out of Afghanistan.

But the Americans just couldn't be satisfied with that. Of course, they felt something was owed to them for sending their CIA representatives to the mujahideen camps secreted in the heart of the Afghan mountains. They felt this gave them the right to speak to the type of government that should be set up in Afghanistan, and when the Taliban regime resisted, the Americans went away. However, it was not to be a permanent departure, and after the attacks against their World Trade Center and Pentagon, they saw an opportunity they could exploit.

The demonstrations themselves had been successful, because al Qaeda had managed to show the infidels they weren't so vulnerable, and that their pathetic airline security was not enough to stop the brave Islamic people.

Now there was paranoia in this faithless and sinful country, and once again Rhatib was going to show them just how easy it was to seize control of their defense systems. The best part was that the Carnivore architecture was going to help him do it. He was going to turn the programs of the FBI against the American people. And he was going to do it right under their noses.

Rhatib turned suddenly at the sound of a door banging followed by heavy footsteps descending the metal staircase leading from the Garden of Allah. Rhatib had been hidden away here for the past few months, unable to go outside even to stretch his legs. He wasn't a prisoner. He would gladly sacrifice for the causes of the New Islamic Front. Nonetheless, the final part of the plan would have to be conducted from their base in the mountains bordering Pakistan, and that would mean he'd be leaving soon.

The source of the footsteps finally came into view, his lumbering reminiscent of man during the Neanderthal period. He wore a long, gray-streaked beard with matching tufts of hair that protruded from beneath his turban, and was dressed in the traditional garb approved by the Taliban regime. His name was Khayyat Malik and he was one of the most dangerous and brave men Rhatib had ever known. He was also lethal and assigned as personal bodyguard and chief of tactical operations for Rhatib.

Rhatib's safety and nurturing were the sole concerns of his uncle, a survivor of the U.S. invasion force in Afghanistan. His uncle was in hiding, and expecting his nephew to join him as soon Rhatib's mission was complete. Rhatib missed his only living relative, but he knew it wasn't safe for them to be together, at least not until he'd accomplished his mission against the Americans.

Malik lumbered to where Rhatib sat and clapped the young prodigy on the back. "How are you, Sadiq?"

"How else would I be?" Rhatib said, snapping a little more harshly than he'd intended. "I've been unable to leave this dungeon since I arrived. To go so long without fresh air is not good for my health."

Malik laughed in his usual good-natured but hoarse tone and replied, "This is not good for anyone. But you will be happy with the news I've brought. It is time for you to leave."

"Leave for where?"

"I am going to take you back home."

"But I'm not finished here," Rhatib protested. "We cannot afford to leave now. It could compromise everything I've worked for."

"Can you not accomplish the rest of your work at the base?"

"Of course I can, but—"

"Then you must do it there. Your uncle insists that we leave. There is a danger…a very real danger from which I must protect you. I've sworn this to your uncle on my blood and the blood of my forefathers."

Rhatib smiled and rested a hand on his faithful servant's shoulder. "I know that you and your family have sworn an oath to the protection of our people. This is your line and your heritage. And it is your reward and the reason for the continued promise of eternity with Allah. However, you must learn patience, my friend. Not everything should be perceived as a threat."

"This is correct," Malik replied pointing toward the ceiling. "But this threat was just above your head last night. And there was shooting and several of our most trusted servants are now dead!"

Rhatib could barely believe what he was hearing, but he trusted Malik. Of course, he wouldn't have heard any such thing, because his underground home was absolutely soundproof. Sensors built into the walls prevented the planting of bugs, and the access door to the basement was hidden in a wall of the janitor's closet, its existence known only to a very select few.

"You feel it is that serious?" Rhatib asked.

Malik nodded and said, "I *know* it is that serious. We must get out of this country. I would advise you pack whatever you need. We leave tonight."

6

Mack Bolan decided to take Tyra MacEwan back to his D.C. hotel. He was certain she would be safe there, and could work in anonymity since she hadn't been with him when he checked in. He sent her ahead with the room key and watched for any observers as she entered the hotel. He followed three minutes later.

MacEwan admitted him to the room on an arranged signal, and once they were settled, Bolan called the desk clerk and asked if a package had been left for him. Why, yes, as a matter of fact one had just arrived by courier, the clerk told him. He would be happy to have someone deliver it. Bolan declined the offer, telling them he'd come for it.

The Executioner returned to his room with a large, plainly wrapped box sent by Kurtzman. He opened it and sorted through the contents, nodding with satisfaction when he saw it contained everything he'd requested. Bear always came through in a pinch.

The box contained two extra clips for the Beretta, along with a few boxes of 9 mm subsonic cartridges that proved so invaluable for soft probes. Bolan expected to encounter a full complement of them this night. Additionally, there was a device Kurtzman had promised for MacEwan's exclusive use: a small electronic gadget that she could attach to her notebook. Bolan didn't know exactly how it worked, but Kurtzman had explained it was similar to a hardware firewall, which would scramble MacEwan's protocol addresses and mask her connections to the Internet. Moreover, she would be dialing into Stony Man computers, which Kurtzman could monitor for any attempted intrusions on her system, while simultaneously collecting the same information MacEwan did.

"Here," Bolan said, handing the small device to MacEwan as she was setting up her notebook system on the table. "My people said to put this between your system and the phone line." He reached into his pocket, withdrew a piece of paper and added, "Then configure your system to dial into this number with these settings. My guy on the other end said you would know how to do this."

"Why do I need this?" she said, studying the little boxlike receptacle with interest.

"So they can't find you again."

MacEwan studied him a moment with an expression that said she still didn't fully trust him. Finally, she nodded and attached the device without argument. If she had to choose sides, she was going to choose Bolan's, and the Executioner was glad for that.

Brognola had suggested it might be better for Bolan to turn protection duties over to Stony Man, but Bolan immediately dismissed the notion. MacEwan was the only one who could help him find the source of the NIF hackers. Eventually, he would track down whoever was behind the penetration of the Carnivore system and take care of business, but until he did, MacEwan was much more valuable to him where he could keep an eye on her. She was the most familiar with Fowler's work, which made her doubly useful in that regard. Not to

mention the fact that Bolan trusted no one else at this stage
of the game to protect her.

For the moment, she would be safe.

"I have to leave for a while," Bolan said suddenly.

MacEwan looked at him with surprise and what looked like
a tinge of panic. "Why?"

"I've got business with the NIF. I laid a tracking device on
one of their people. I'm going to see where it leads me."

Bolan went to the bathroom, stripped from his clothes and
took a quick shower. As the hot spray washed away the smell
of gunfire and sweat, he thought about his situation. He was
caught between mission objectives, and it bothered the hell
out of him. He'd been here before, yeah. But that didn't
change his mission. He had to take the offensive while still
trying to protect MacEwan and prevent any further compromise in Carnivore. That latter objective was the hardest.

How do you fight an enemy you can't see, soldier?

It was difficult enough to fight a war on two fronts, especially when one was purely offensive and the other defensive.
No military tactician in his right mind would have tested such
odds. But Bolan was different in this regard, and he had always believed that fate favored those who were best prepared
for it.

As he toweled himself dry, the Executioner reconsidered
his options. It would have been nice to get MacEwan off his
hands, but he couldn't be persuaded by mere convenience.
Hell, when had his War Everlasting ever been convenient?
The very idea was laughable. As far as he was concerned,
he couldn't back off the enemy either and hope the whole
thing just blew over. If there were more holes, and Kurtzman or MacEwan couldn't plug them fast enough, more di-

rect means would be required. The only way to do that was to put the perpetrators on the run and keep them that way. So, in many ways the decision had already been made for him. Once again, fate and destiny had control of the situation, and it was up to Bolan to simply see it through to its conclusion.

"Are you hungry?" Bolan asked after dressing in his black-suit and withdrawing his weapons carrier from beneath the bed.

MacEwan started to shake her head, but then thought better of it and nodded. Bolan ordered some sandwiches from room service.

He pulled a small pistol from the case and checked the action before handing the weapon butt first to MacEwan. "You know how to use this?" he asked.

She took the pistol immediately, studied it a moment, and then nodded as she set it on the table. "Walther P-5, right?"

Bolan nodded. "You know your guns."

"My father was into them." She looked up and met his gaze, adding, "Of course, not quite as much as you seem to be."

"Guns are tools, just like anything else. They're useful in the right hands, destructive in the wrong ones."

"And by 'the right hands' I suppose you mean yours," she said.

Bolan shrugged with a cool expression. "Those are your words, not mine. I kill out of necessity and duty, and nothing more."

"It would appear I offended you. Sorry."

"My skin's thick, lady. It's going to take more than that to hurt my feelings."

"It usually doesn't take long for me to rub most people the wrong way," she admitted.

Bolan nodded. "Looks like we have something in common then."

He returned to his work, unrolling a rag on the bed and setting the Desert Eagle next to it within easy reach. He quickly stripped and cleaned the Beretta, and reassembled it before replacing it in his shoulder leather. He loaded three spare clips for the Beretta, and one additional magazine for the Desert Eagle.

Finally, Bolan withdrew the last pieces of hardware he would need: four M-67 fragmentation grenades and an FNC assault rifle. He loaded the carbine and stowed a couple of extra 30-round magazines in the hip pockets of his black combat fatigues.

After the sandwiches arrived, Bolan and MacEwan ate mechanically without talking. When they were finished, the soldier donned a military web belt with a holster, dropped the Desert Eagle into place and finally zipped the bag closed before shrugging into his overcoat.

"You'll be okay here until I get back. Don't answer the door, don't call anyone, no room service. I'll hang out the Do Not Disturb sign and leave my key with the front desk. Understood?"

She nodded with an almost blank expression. As Bolan opened the door she said, "Hey, Cooper, I really am sorry for what I said before. I guess I owe you my life."

Bolan nodded and replied, "Forget it."

He was out the door.

THE TRACKING DEVICE worked perfectly, its homing signal spitting coordinates on the screen that made it easy for Bolan to follow.

Chalk up another success for Hermann Schwarz. The Able

Team electronics wizard was a genius in his own right—earning him the nickname Gadgets—and an expert in electronic surveillance and countersurveillance. The Executioner almost wished he had all three hard cases of Able Team with him. The support would have been a nice change. Still, Bolan knew he had to go it alone on this one...at least for now.

The transmitter sewn into the lining of the coat he'd loaned to Fadilah emitted a signal that led Bolan right back to the Garden of Allah. This was a big surprise, especially considering the amount of attention they probably received from local law enforcement after Bolan's first visit. The soldier considered this turn of events as he studied the front of the club.

Initially, the Executioner had considered trying for another soft probe, given the early-morning hours. However, three armed Arabs, accompanied by a fourth man who was either American or European, canceled that idea. That was another oddity, seeing a white face in that crowd. Okay, so there was a better than offside chance the NIF had American contacts, possibly even members belonging to American business or organized crime concerns. Bolan wasn't about to stereotype. What he planned to do this time was hit the gunmen hard and fast.

The street was essentially deserted, and Bolan decided if he was going to do it, now was as good a time as any. The Executioner shrugged out of his coat, checked the action of the FNC as he brought it into battery, then left the sedan and crossed the cold, wet street. He angled toward the quartet, his ghostly, wraithlike form quickly narrowing the distance between him and those who would be the first casualties of his frontal assault.

They hardly realized they were under attack until he was on them.

The closest guard's head exploded as Bolan raised the FNC on the run and triggered a short burst from less than ten yards. Blood, bone and brain matter splattered onto the tough standing next to him, who died under a similar burst to the stomach and chest.

The third gunman managed to produce a mini-Uzi from under his very American suit jacket, but his aim was off due to the conflicting objective of self-preservation. Bolan fired a sustained burst, moving the muzzle of the weapon in a corkscrew pattern. The high-velocity rounds blew flesh from extremities as well as penetrating vital organs. The gunman's torn and bleeding body did a pirouette before collapsing to the pavement.

Bolan managed to hit the ground as the surviving white man hastily capped off two rounds from a stainless-steel .45-caliber weapon. Bolan rolled to a kneeling position, steadied the FNC and shot the pistol cleanly from the man's hand. The guy flashed a shocked look, realizing his only means of defense had just been decimated. He turned and yanked on the club door, but a viselike hand grabbed the back of his collar and stopped him short.

"What's the rush?" Bolan asked, and then he put his foot out to stop the closing door as he shoved the man through the vestibule. The guy's face contacted the inside door, breaking his nose, knocking out a front tooth and leaving a bloody face print as evidence of the ordeal.

Bolan withdrew the Beretta and pressed its cold muzzle against the back of the man's head. "I'm having a lot of trouble controlling my temper where you're concerned."

The guy was having trouble talking with the side of his face mashed against the door. "You kill me, you'll be sorry, you mother—"

Bolan cuffed him with the butt of the Beretta. "Shut up."

"You know who you're dealing with here, man?"

The Executioner replied, "Yeah, you're nothing but a group of thugs who get their kicks killing Americans. So I know your kind and I exterminate them." Bolan pressed the muzzle of the Beretta tighter against the man's head and continued, "Now, I'm going to ask questions, you're going to answer them."

"Piss off!" the man squealed as blood began to ooze from his scalp where Bolan had removed some skin with his pistol butt.

The Executioner ignored the outburst. "Your friends outside…are they NIF?"

At first, the guy remained silent, but a prod from the Beretta made him realize that Bolan wouldn't hesitate to put a bullet in his brain. "Yes!"

"Four days ago, an American scientist named Fowler was sniped right in front of the FBI. Who pulled the trigger?"

"I don't know."

Bolan tapped him with the Beretta. "Try again."

"N-no, I meant that w-we did it, but I don't know *who* did it. I don't know who pulled the trigger."

"What's your interest here?" Bolan demanded to know.

"I represent Mr. Lenzini."

"Lenzini? You mean Nicolas Lenzini?" Bolan asked.

The guy nodded.

Bolan believed his prisoner, but he was still intrigued by the answer. Nicolas Lenzini—of the Washington Lenzinis— was a favorite son in the most powerful organized crime Family in the nation's capital. The Lenzinis had a long history running the numbers games in D.C., an area on which they held the monopoly. No one in the city placed or collected on a bet without the okay of the Lenzinis, and Nicolas was the chief enforcer and bag collection side of the Family.

Whether horse racing, football, or payment so local cops looked the other way, Nicolas Lenzini controlled money movement, laundering and black bag operations throughout the city and surrounding suburbs. In fact, Lenzini controlled numbers all up and down the majority of the East Coast, and was notorious for killing anyone who got in his way. But something about Lenzini being involved with Islamic terrorists just didn't wash.

"What's his interest in this?" Bolan asked.

"I don't know," he said. "I'm just supposed to keep an eye on some whiz kid they've got working for them. I swear that's all I know."

"What kind of whiz kid?"

"Like that Fed techie, man," the guy replied. "Some kind of genius with computers, or something. I don't know, okay? What the fuck you want from me?"

"Where's this kid now?" Bolan demanded to know.

"They took him," he replied. "I don't know where, so don't ask."

"Where were they hiding him?"

The guy managed to gesture toward the inside of the building. Bolan grabbed him by the collar and pulled him off the door. He ordered the guy to open it and then shoved him through the doorway into the darkened interior. The hood led him to the recessed door from which Bolan had entered the night before, and then down the hallway to the door that had been locked from the outside.

"Open it."

"I don't have a key, man."

"What's behind it?" Bolan asked.

"It leads to a basement. That's where they were hiding the kid."

"Was this kid a willing party or prisoner?"

"I don't have a clue, pal. Okay? He was Arab or Muslim, or somethin', ya know? Look, all I know is Mr. Lenzini put up some cash to build some sweet setup in the basement of this dive so the kid had some place to work. Now it's all gone to shit. They figured out somebody was on to them, and they split. I stayed on and acted dumb, 'cause Mr. Lenzini's got a lot riding on this. I just do what I'm told, okay? I'm here to protect the boss's investment."

The Executioner's tone was taunting. "Yeah, you're just a poor, underpaid lackey."

The sound of footsteps on stairs resounded in the hallway. It was coming from behind the door and getting louder. Bolan knocked the butt of the pistol behind the hood's ear and lowered his body to the ground, leaving it to rest against the heavy door. He stood to the side and pressed his back to the wall, holding the Beretta at the ready.

The door opened a moment later, and a very large Arab man pushed on the door, grunting with the effort of trying to move the unconscious hood's weight. He stuck his head through the door and peered around the corner looking down to see what was blocking his exit, totally oblivious to the Executioner's presence. He looked into the muzzle of the Beretta 93-R milliseconds before Bolan squeezed the trigger. The guy's head snapped back and the back of his skull exploded from the bone-crushing force of the bullet. A loud, boisterous voice called out inquisitively in Arabic. There was a second party behind the first, probably inquiring as to the delay.

Bolan leaned against the door to hold the body up while he reached down and hauled his prisoner away from the door. He grabbed the nearly headless corpse by the shirt and lifted him upright before opening the door. The dark-skinned man coming up the stairs had a cardboard box balanced precariously on one shoulder, and his eyes widened when he saw the Executioner standing in the open doorway. Bolan heaved the dead man at his cohort, and both bodies tumbled down the steep stairwell.

The Executioner followed in close pursuit, holstering the Beretta and bringing the FNC into the ready position. He reached the landing and jumped over the two bodies that had come to rest there, leaping into a large open space filled with an electronics workstation in varying degrees of disassembly. Two more workers stood at the station, tools in hand, staring at the black-clad warrior with stark surprise. After their initial shock, they reacted but Bolan didn't give them any quarter. The Executioner triggered the FNC, dispatching the terrorists quickly with two short bursts.

After a search of the basement, Bolan located his coat stashed in a nearby locker. He moved over to a wide desk that was missing a monitor or other output. A cursory inspection, however, revealed a tower beneath the table; it probably contained hard drives or other removable disks with valuable information. Kurtzman would definitely want a look at this stuff, and Bolan knew it might even contain clues leading to this mysterious kid who was allegedly working with the New Islamic Front using monies supplied by one of the most influential and connected organized crime families in the country.

Bolan scooped the computer tower case under his arm and climbed the stairs. He stopped at the landing and looked down as Lenzini's hired gun groaned and slowly rubbed the back of his head. The man looked at the small amount of blood on his palm, then groaned again.

Bolan said, "What's that kid's name?"

"I don't remember, asshole," the hood replied. "It was weird...uh, Rat-something. Shit, I don't know."

"Today's your lucky day," Bolan said. "I want you to carry a message back to Lenzini."

"What?"

"You tell him no more playing footsies with the New Islamic Front. You tell him the NIF's going to get burned to the ground, and if he sticks with them, he'll burn too. I don't have time to deal with him now, but I'm going to make sure the FBI gets wind it was *him* responsible for Fowler's death."

"Damn, man, have you lost a nut? I go back and tell Lenzini that, he's going to know I talked. First, he'll rip off my nads with pliers, and then he'll kill me. And then he'll kill my family."

"He's going to be too busy protecting all of his games in town to worry about a peon like you. You just give him my message. You got it?" Bolan said.

"Yeah," the guy mumbled. "I got it."

The Executioner hauled the guy to his feet and showed him out the back door, then retrieved the computer and headed for the front door. As he passed through the club, Bolan primed an M-67 frag and tossed it into the rows of liquor bottles stacked behind the bar. The grenade exploded and ignited the flammable liquid. Bolan knew no more terror would be dealt from the Garden of Allah, because he'd just turned this oasis into a desert.

And on his next offense, he planned to destroy forever the organization's very existence.

7

Stony Man Farm, Virginia

Within a few hours of receiving Bolan's package, Aaron Kurtzman had extracted quite a bit of information from the two hard drives left inside the computer. Brognola and Price were quite pleased to hear it, and they immediately contacted the Executioner to update him on the situation.

"We've got good news, Striker," Brognola began.

"There must be some mistake," Bolan said.

The group couldn't refrain from enjoying a bit of laughter at the Executioner's dry retort.

Brognola continued, "Bear managed to disseminate the information on that package you sent us, so I'll let him fill you in on the details. In the meantime, I had Barb look into the joint research project of Fowler and MacEwan. Barb, fill him in on what you know."

Price cleared her throat with a nod. "I don't know how much MacEwan has told you, so sorry if I'm redundant."

"Actually, she hasn't told me much," Bolan interjected. "I don't think she totally trusts me yet."

"Sounds like maybe the feeling's mutual, Striker," Brognola said.

"Yeah."

"Well," Price continued, "it was difficult to crack Fowler's security, but Aaron came through, and boy was it an eye-opener. About seven years ago, Justice contracted a joint study commission composed of members from DARPA, MIT and Carnegie-Mellon Law School to evaluate Carnivore. They were to determine if the system provided investigators with only the information defined by the parameters of electronic surveillance warrants, risked any impairment of private, commercial, or corporate networks, and whether there were liabilities the system might incur in the area of security breaches. It took them more than a year to complete that study, and several more until the results were made public. And I have to say that the system was described in considerable detail."

"In enough detail that one or two top-notch hackers might be able to crack its security?" Bolan asked.

"I can't say for sure, but Bear seems to think so," Price said, looking in Kurtzman's direction.

The Stony Man cyberwizard added, "We're not completely sure where this hacker working for the NIF got his information, but based on the files I *could* crack, he obviously did his homework. Most of the reference material we found on Carnivore is in English."

"So we have to assume this information is American based," Bolan concluded. "So much for security."

"Wherever the NIF got its information," Price continued, "it made the most of it. I think that Dr. Fowler discovered someone was trying to break into the system. My NSA contacts think that's the reason they killed him, and it's probably why they're trying to kill MacEwan."

"Two gorillas were beating on her when I arrived," Bolan

replied. "She told me they were asking her a lot of questions about Fowler's research."

"How did MacEwan get into this in the first place?" Brognola asked.

"She was on loan by DARPA, at Fowler's request, and temporarily assigned to his team to reinvestigate some of the findings in the study that seemed off," Price said.

"So Fowler had some familiarity with her?" Brognola asked.

"MacEwan is an MIT graduate, as you already know. It seems she based her graduate thesis on the study findings, criticizing them and citing the results as incomplete and superficial. Well, Fowler had apparently always been a strong opponent of Carnivore, and naturally he picked MacEwan to help him prove that it was neither mature nor secure enough to implement in the public sector."

"Okay," Bolan said, "so Fowler gets MacEwan to help him prove Carnivore isn't as secure as the FBI would like the public to think. That made him a liability to both the NIF and the FBI."

"You're thinking somebody inside might have killed him?"

"Maybe they didn't pull the trigger," Bolan replied, "but one of our own might have told the NIF where and when to hit him."

"I'll start running down those angles through my people at Justice," Brognola said. "In the meantime, is there anything else you have for us, Barb?"

"Not too much beyond that, although there's some technical details I know Aaron wants to discuss."

Brognola nodded at Kurtzman.

"Striker, I'll keep it brief, but all I can say for right now is to keep your eyes and ears open. First, I can tell you that Carnivore is deficient when it comes to protecting the integrity of information it collects. When FBI personnel install computers at an Internet service provider location, those computers come under the control of that ISP. There's nothing other than the physical security measures at these locations to stop someone from tampering with the host computers. Now, there's no interface on these computers, like a monitor or anything else, but traffic could easily be rerouted by ISP personnel under the payroll of NIF."

"So you're saying that this could be happening anywhere in this country, and you're not yet sure where," Bolan said.

"Well, we're still working on the routing side of it. Understand that there are billions of miles of cable through which we have to trace, and retrace our little electronic steps," Kurtzman explained. "That's going to take some time, even for my team. But we do know that they're taking whoever worked this system out of the country tonight. I managed to crack an e-mail that was sent in Arabic. I had it translated and will read it to you. 'Uncle, have not finished my work here, but Khayyat insists that we return to the compound tonight. I will contact you as soon as we are safely out of American airspace. Allah be with you, Sadiq.'"

"Interesting," Bolan said.

"We thought so, as well," Kurtzman replied. "We're running that name through every terrorist profile we have now, but so far no flags. Our records have only one known terrorist named Sadiq who worked with the Armed Islamic Group and is confirmed dead. Plus, the profile doesn't fit for NIF operations."

"Yeah, wrong region entirely," Bolan said. "I've done a lot of business with the GIA and they've always seemed to confine the majority of their activities to Africa. I know they've worked with al Qaeda in the past, but this doesn't seem like their way of doing things."

"You believe the NIF is working totally on its own here, Striker?" Price asked.

"I'm not sure yet. But if they are getting outside help, I'm sure it's not coming from the GIA. There's some other game going here. I'd start checking into flights out of here tonight, official and unofficial. Look for anything that might be headed toward Europe or Asia. All domestic and international flights into or out of the U.S. are required to file a full flight plan, including private charters, if they don't want to get shot out of the sky. That message mentioned American airspace, and I'd be willing to bet they'll register their flight to avoid suspicion."

"Agreed," Brognola said. "Bear, if you find anything you think out of the ordinary, why don't you work with MacEwan to send those transponder codes and radio frequencies? After all, she's the most qualified at spotting this guy's work. Maybe she'll find a way to track him."

"I'll get on it right away," Kurtzman said.

"Sounds good," Bolan said. "And I've got one other favor to ask. One of the hitters I ran into at that NIF club was part of Nicolas Lenzini's crew."

"The numbers runner?" Brognola asked with a bit of incredulity.

"The same."

"How's he involved in this?"

"That's what I don't know," Bolan said. "Can you guys dig into his most recent activities and let me know what you find?"

Brognola replied, "We'll get on it pronto. In the meantime, you watch yourself, Striker."

"Always." With that, the line went dead.

The Stony Man threesome looked at one another, and all knew what the others were thinking. The Executioner was about to light a fire under the NIF that might also smoke out the kingpin of the Washington underworld. All hell was about to break loose.

And Mack Bolan was carrying the torch.

WHEN THE EXECUTIONER got back to the hotel, he was surprised to find Tyra MacEwan tucked under the covers, fast asleep. He tried to be quiet as he stripped out of his gear, but the rattling of the weaponry caused her to stir. She opened her eyes and looked at him, an expression of fright at first, but then she relaxed when her groggy consciousness told her it was Bolan.

"You're still alive," she said in a soft, sleepy voice.

"And you're still here," he replied.

Bare, sensuous shoulders peeked out from the blankets and shrugged ever so slightly. "That's no surprise. Even if I decided to leave, where would I go? There's not a lot of people I can trust, and I don't really think it's a good idea to put what friends I do have at risk of getting shot, blown up, or otherwise having their lives disrupted with what amounts to nothing more than my own stupidity."

Bolan finished depositing the last of his heavy weaponry in his bag and pulled up a chair next to the bed. The lights of the motel parking lot streamed through the satiny, thin curtains, and MacEwan's face seemed to glow under them. She was distractingly beautiful, but the Executioner could not let himself succumb to that beauty. It could prove fatal to both of them if the warrior let down his guard, even if for a stolen moment of passion.

"Listen up, Tyra," Bolan said, glancing sternly at her.

"What's happened isn't your fault. It's not anybody's fault. That's just the way it is."

MacEwan appeared defiant, but it was apparent she saw something in the Executioner's visage that was almost frightening. Bolan exuded an air of authority, but sitting there in that chair, in that moment—smelling of blood and spent gunpowder and violence—he also exuded an air of brutal death.

"Men like you must know very little peace, Cooper. It must be like some continuous torment, never being able to relax…even for a moment. Not being able to know love or peace or a sense of home. Seems like a horrible, lonely existence."

"It can be," Bolan replied. "But most of the time, it is what is, which all comes down to what I make of it. There are a great many people in the world who can't live my kind of life, and fight my kind of war. But I know a few who still do it…men I've fought next to. I've waded through the worst, and they've followed me to hell and back, and I'm grateful for every damned one of them."

"Camaraderie and friendship are things I understand," she said. "Killing and bloodshed aren't."

"You're saying you think I'm a killer."

"I'm saying that I don't understand why you don't find more peaceful methods. It's not up to me to judge you, or what you do. I'm just grateful to be alive, and because you've given me no reason not to so far, I'm going to trust you. I just hope I'm not wrong."

"You're not," he said with a smile. "Let's kill all this grim reaper stuff. I need you up and dressed and hooked up. I've got a mission, and we think we may have discovered who's behind all of this."

"That's good enough news for me!" she said. She slid out

of bed on the opposite side, conscious of the fact Bolan was still looking at her. She wrapped herself in the sheet, looking a bit embarrassed. She smiled shyly, picked up her clothes, walked rapidly to the bathroom and closed the door.

Bolan smiled, shook his head, got up and made coffee. When he heard the shower go on, he decided it was safe enough for him to strip out of his black fatigues and get into something less combat-oriented. He was dressed in new denims and a flannel shirt, and sitting at the table enjoying a hot cup of strong, black java by the time MacEwan was out of the shower.

The technologist joined him at the table and immediately went to work signing into her laptop. Bolan put his chair in such a position that he could watch what she was doing. He indicated toward his cup in way of offering her some, but she shook her head while keeping both eyes on the screen.

"Are you computer literate?" she asked, looking doubtful.

"I've used a few in my time," Bolan replied truthfully, "but I wouldn't classify myself an expert. I understand them enough to get by, and I figure I'll leave all of the other stuff to people like you."

"That's better than many," she said. "A lot of people hate computers. Probably because they don't understand them."

"Makes sense. I'd say that's why a lot of people hate anything."

As she finished signing on, and hooked up to the secure but restricted gateway Kurtzman had set up for her through the Stony Man network, she said, "I think I've finally figured out what's going on. The system your people have me into is incredibly sophisticated. I saw some things I've never seen used quite so effectively like software-based routers and IP address rerouters. Makes your network very secure and damned near foolproof. Yes, sir, quite an impressive setup indeed."

"The person in charge of it has been doing this awhile," Bolan said.

"I don't doubt it," she replied.

"So, you were saying you found out something about our little hacker?" Bolan said.

"Actually, it took some time and interactive sessions with your guy who calls himself 'Bear,' but we did get pretty deep into Mitch's files. I found some algorithms behind his programs, and your friend used a scripting language to decode them." She fixed him with a suspicious expression and added, "A scripting language the likes of which I've never seen before. Complicated and based on what looks like assembly programming."

"Is that significant to you?" Bolan asked.

"You could say that. Assembly languages are obsolete, tedious and very complicated, but 'Bear' did it as if it were nothing."

"You can stop probing," Bolan said. "I'm not discussing my people any further. Now, you want to tell me what you've found?"

She nodded slowly and then turned her attention to the notebook screen. A moment later, she opened a file and showed him a series of multicolored lines. "These are bandwidth transmissions that we were finally able to trace to their source. It looks like Mitch knew something was up months ago. His personal log says it took him nearly four weeks, but he was eventually able to trace the original signals inside the Carnivore system back to the area around south Washington."

Bolan nodded. "They were coming from a club called the

Garden of Allah. There is a faction of terrorists called the New Islamic Front who've been operating a nationwide network inside the country for the past few years. Recently, they smuggled in a technology expert, some sort of whiz kid from the intelligence I've gathered, and he helped them crack the security on Carnivore."

"But you don't know how yet," MacEwan interjected.

"No, we don't. What I do think is that the NIF felt it an important enough secret that they would shut up anyone they suspected knew anything about it."

"So they killed Mitchell and then planned to kill me," she said, shuddering.

"Yeah."

"But that's what I don't understand," MacEwan said. "Why not just kill me? Why beat me and ask me questions?"

"First they needed to know if you talked to anyone else," Bolan replied matter-of-factly.

MacEwan nodded then, her expression betraying the realization of the horrors she might have endured had the Executioner not arrived when he did. "Well, there is one thing I discovered just before I dropped off to sleep."

She tapped a key and all of the lines disappeared but one, a very faint yellowish line that was more distorted and transparent than the other ones he'd seen. "This is a signal that was buried under the rest. The computer displays it differently because it's special."

"In what way?" Bolan asked.

"Well, in my business we call this a phantom signal. Under most frequency modulations, it's virtually invisible because the standard frequency signals most expect to see bury these phantom ones. Even if it were filtered out, a lot of Internet security advisers would just call it noise or echo. I think even Mitchell didn't catch it. But I think this is the signal these hackers used to get inside of Carnivore. The evidence I've found so far tells me that the signal doesn't have a source here in the United States, but rather a source from another region of the world entirely."

"So let me see if I understand this," Bolan interjected. "You're saying this signal didn't originate here, it originated from some other country, but you're not yet sure where."

"Exactly."

"Okay, so they inserted a phantom frequency and rode on that. I'm with you so far. But that doesn't explain how they got inside Carnivore's security."

"Actually it does," MacEwan countered, "but not in a way I would ever have thought possible."

Bolan was already amazed at MacEwan's technical knowledge, and now she was astounding him further. She typed furiously at the keyboard, and as he studied her beautiful profile, he realized he was looking at nothing less than a female version of Kurtzman. The woman was truly brilliant—there was no other way to describe her—and the Executioner had a sneaking suspicion that she was going to prove herself an invaluable ally when the chips were down.

When she finished typing and tapped a function key on her portable system, a simple but colorful picture was displayed on the computer screen.

"All computers that are connected to the Internet, whether directly or through corporate or virtual private networks, must communicate through one or more types of protocols. These protocols are based on what's known as the Open Systems Interconnection, or OSI, model you see here," MacEwan explained.

"Simply put, OSI is a worldwide standard communications architecture that describes how any protocol usually occurs in seven layers. Protocol control gets passed from one layer to the next, starting with the Application Layer, which most just call Layer 7. The signal then moves to Layer 6, then 5, and so forth. When the signals riding on a given protocol reach their destination, they return up the OSI hierarchy in reverse order."

"Sounds complicated," Bolan said.

"It's not really if you understand what's happening at each layer, and can tie it to that thing the average joe interfaces with that we call a computer. For example, you send e-mail or transfer a file to someone. That's considered Layer 7. When you actually send it, the computer first encrypts the data and then converts it from whatever language it's presently in, such as ASCII or EBCDIC, to the binary language understood by computers. A session is then opened with the network or ISP, there's a communications handshake, the message is sent, and then networks all over the country route and reroute the message in packets until it reaches its final destination. This communication is in electrical signals, transported through cables, which are the signals you saw represented graphically just a minute ago."

"So our hackers used those signals to get inside Carnivore?" Bolan asked.

"Apparently. Where this is something totally new is that up until now, it was theoretically impossible for any data packets to be streamed through a system unless there were some kind of acknowledgment between computers. Most information technology systems analysts and managers rely on firewalls to block any unwanted traffic. Apparently, your terrorist friends have found some other way to crack this functionality, and now they're inside Carnivore. If they can get into and out of corporate or private systems without detection, God help us. They could already have full control of Carnivore right now, and they're just waiting for some perfect opportunity to throw the proverbial switch." MacEwan sighed.

"What could they do with it?" Bolan asked.

"Shit, Cooper!" she said with a fresh realization that resulted in an expression of horror. "Carnivore has the ability to tie into just about anything, particularly monitoring of government networks and Department of Defense computers. If they really wanted to, they could take control of our defense grids, monitor our most sensitive communications, control troop and equipment movements…the possibilities are endless!"

The Executioner turned, looked toward the window and replied, "Then I guess I've got my work cut out for me."

8

Once MacEwan got hooked up with Kurtzman, it didn't take long for them to get a handle on the enemy. The problem for Bolan was formulating a plan that would have favorable results. He had to neutralize any enemy defenses, grab the fabled prize whiz kid—if there even was one—and get out with his head intact.

To the Executioner, that was all in a day's work.

There was only one flight Stony Man intelligence could conclude met all the criteria. If Bear was wrong, his efforts this night would be for naught. But Bolan had confidence that the Stony Man cybernetics genius was right on the money. Kurtzman's intuition told him it reeked of an NIF operation, and the Executioner had to agree.

The flight was scheduled to depart just after midnight. It was a Gulfstream IV-SP, supposedly a round-trip charter for six passengers, with a final destination of Rio de Janeiro via one stop in Mexico City for refueling. Kurtzman wasn't buying it, and neither was Mack Bolan. That was an unusual route, at best, and the normal flight plan for a private charter jet of that type and range would have called for a straight shot. An expert had advised that the fuel capacity of that make provided enough range to get across the Atlantic.

Under questioning by FBI, the charter company advised that the deposit and final trip costs had been paid via a cashier's check, and that the renter had promised any monies owed at the end of the flight in cash. They had also promised that a list of passengers would be provided upon their arrival, and not earlier, citing that the "sensitive nature of their business prohibited disclosure any earlier than that."

Way too suspicious, and Bolan was on it. He broke from his study of the airfield ahead of him long enough to check his watch: twenty minutes before takeoff. The flight crew had arrived and was obviously engaged in preflight checks, but there was still no sign of the terrorists. The Executioner could only hope he'd guessed correctly. After all, it had occurred to him that even if this were the NIF, it was entirely possible they had engineered the entire thing to throw any observers off the track.

If life had taught Bolan anything, it was to never underestimate the enemy. This enemy was particularly unpredictable, with the knowledge and resources necessary to counter even the best and most effective antiterrorist tactics. Still, those who operated inside an organization such as the New Islamic Front could become lackadaisical when allowed to operate too long domestically. And it had become increasingly difficult to smuggle people into the country, let alone the various weapons of destruction at their disposal.

However, it was more difficult to stop computers because they controlled nearly everything. Bolan could see the brilliance and terror in the NIF's plan. He had to shut it down; he couldn't blow it.

"What exactly are we waiting for?" MacEwan asked him.

He turned and looked at her, realizing he'd been lost in his own thoughts and had probably been too quiet. "From the information you gave my people, we think that the NIF is going to attempt to get this hacker out of the country tonight."

"How?"

Bolan inclined his head toward the plane and replied, "On that."

"You know, I could have stayed at the motel while you did this," she said.

The Executioner shook his head. "No, it was time to move you. I trust our security measures, but not to such a degree that I'm comfortable with keeping you in one place for too long."

"Do you mean to convince me that I'm safer running around the East Coast and confronting terrorists directly than sitting in some little motel nobody even probably cares about?"

"Yes," he replied.

She studied him a moment longer with her usual expression of skepticism before responding, "Whatever you say, Cooper."

"I know it doesn't make sense to you," Bolan said, "but you're going to have to trust me on this. You're worth a hell of a lot to me alive, sure, but to the NIF you're worth even more dead. I don't have a field resource available right now with your technical expertise. Until I nail these bastards, I want you within arm's reach."

She looked out the rain-speckled windshield and said, "Can't we turn on the heat?"

Bolan shook his head. "Someone might see the exhaust."

"Well, it's going to fog up pretty quickly, and then you aren't going to be able to see anything."

"Then I'll stand in the rain," he said.

"You do have a singular wit, Cooper. You know that?"

"I've never heard that before."

"I'll bet. You—"

"Wait a minute," Bolan cut in. "I think we're in business."

He raised the small, compact binoculars and turned the key to the accessory position to wipe away the rain before focusing on the plane. A group of men had exited the small charter building and were headed toward the plane. Bolan did a quick count: six, with two in the middle flanked by four corners of significant size. They moved like professionals, and the Executioner immediately marked the play as four bodyguards for two VIPs.

"All right," he said, turning to face MacEwan, "you stay here. Keep the doors locked and keep yourself out of sight. If you see me go down, wait five minutes and then split. Get back to Washington as fast as you can, and then call my people. They'll arrange to pick you up. Don't call *anyone* else. Not your mother, not friends, nobody. Otherwise you'll be signing their death warrants. Understood?"

She nodded and opened her mouth to say something else, but Bolan went EVA without giving her the chance to say it. Bolan couldn't allow MacEwan to distract him now; he had to keep his mind on the mission. It was high time he finished his business with the NIF—once and for all.

UNDER THE PROTECTION of nearly a dozen NIF soldiers and the inimitable Khayyat Malik, Rhatib watched intently from an overhang near the terminal as a decoy, accompanied by five additional NIF soldiers, walked toward the plane. Malik had insisted that his men check it out first, and he didn't plan to allow anything to stand in his way of protecting Rhatib.

Rhatib looked up at Malik, who easily towered over him

by a foot or so. His protector was a big man, with dark hair and beard, and equally dark eyes that were always probing, always scrutinizing everything around them.

"Are you sure all of this is necessary?" Rhatib asked.

Malik only nodded.

Rhatib sighed.

Malik suddenly grabbed Rhatib's arm tightly and shoved him backward into the group of NIF bodyguards, who immediately surrounded him.

"I knew it," Malik whispered.

Rhatib was trying to see, but he couldn't get a clear view past the wall of bodies surrounding him. He crouched and finally caught a glimpse of an almost spectral form, attired in black from head to toe, sprinting toward the plane with the grace of a cheetah. Rhatib had seen violence before. He'd even received formal training in the arts of combat. He knew enough to defend himself against most attackers, and he could hold his own even against men the size of Malik.

But there was something about the black angel of death now crossing the tarmac and leveling an automatic weapon at the group near the plane that sent a painful stab of fear through his heart. And Rhatib watched helplessly as the muzzle of the weapon put forth flashes of flame and men—good and brave men of the eternal jihad—began to fall under the sudden and swift onslaught of this pervasive and deadly new enemy.

MACK BOLAN TRIGGERED the FNC, and sent two short fusillades in the direction of the group. One of the NIF crew took the first salvo in the face. Two more shared the second burst, one spinning in place before collapsing to the wet pavement, the other knocked off his feet by two rounds to the chest.

The remaining NIF guard demonstrated an admirable response to the threat, his training evident in both reaction time and movement. The terrorist shouted something to the pair of men he'd been guarding and then shoulder rolled across the tarmac behind cover of one of the plane's struts. The Executioner simultaneously watched for weapons from the pair now searching frantically for cover, but his worry was short-lived as he reached the concealment of an outbuilding just in time to avoid a full burst from the remaining terrorist guard's AKSU.

Bolan had to be careful in picking off his targets, because he wanted the VIPs in the middle alive at any cost short of his own life. If one of the pair was this mysterious hacker, then that individual held information vital to the electronic security of the entire nation. That was *if* Bolan were to believe what MacEwan had told him, and thus far she'd given him no reason to doubt otherwise.

Not to mention, there just plain wasn't anybody else to do it.

Bolan returned another salvo, but it wasn't really an attempt to hit his man as much as keep him pinned down until the warrior could form an alternate plan. He watched for only a moment as the two unarmed VIPs standing in the open, decided to make for the plane. Bolan turned to watch as one of the Gulfstream's crew members poked his head out the door, trying to get a better look at what was going on. One of the pair rushing the plane suddenly produced a pistol from his jacket and shot the man in the head.

Bolan clenched his teeth, biting back the urge to kill the pair there and then. Now the damned civilians were getting blown away, and that wasn't good. It was likely that a lot more people would die if the Executioner didn't make a decision right now.

He did.

Bolan drew the .44 Magnum Desert Eagle in a single, coordinated motion born from years of training and experience. He leveled the shiny hand cannon, and squeezed the trigger. It was a fleeting moment of judgment for the NIF gunman. The bullet took the guy in the back as he was trying to force his way into the plane, shooting randomly at unseen targets. The man arched his back, reaching behind him as if he'd been shot with an arrow and was trying to pull it out. Suddenly unbalanced, he fell backward onto his companion. The two men toppled from the stairs and landed on the tarmac.

Bolan detected sudden movement in his peripheral vision. The Executioner looked to his right and saw nearly a dozen well-armed NIF gunmen advancing on his position. The muzzles of their weapons winked erratically, but there was one massive sound of destruction from their combined reports. Bolan narrowly escaped being ventilated, getting low and listening to the familiar sound of bullets zinging over his head or striking the wooden outbuilding. Pieces of wood, plastic and aluminum rained on his head and back, along with a significant amount of fibrous dust, and the icy ground was cold against his knees and hands.

He wondered where the hell they had come from, but then he realized it had been a trap. After all, the NIF knew about him. Several times already he'd been a target, and now he was still being hunted. But instead of tracking him they had waited until he'd come to them. Somebody who knew what they were doing was controlling the NIF terrorists.

Bolan decided to even the odds a bit, especially if he wanted a fighting chance to get away. As he detached a white phosphorous grenade from his load-bearing gear, he heard the sound of the plane's engines starting. There was no way in hell he'd be able to stop the plane, put down the advancing enemy and get out alive. The most immediate threat requiring his attention was the approaching group of terrorists that was obviously hell-bent on ending it there once and for all. The Executioner would have time to square things away later, but at the moment the priority had to be staying alive. He yanked the pin on the grenade and exposed himself long enough during a lull in the firing to toss the bomb underhanded into the midst of the advancing terrorists.

Many were in the midst of reloading clips when the small and seemingly harmless object landed at their feet. It took a few of them a split second to recognize the device, but the rest just didn't get a good look in time. The area around them suddenly glowed with the explosion, and a moment later Bolan could hear the screaming as the phosphorous exploded on those standing immediately next to the grenade. The chief chemical agent inside the grenade burned on oxygen and did significant damage to tissues in a short period of time. However, the tissue injury was secondary to the ignition of clothing, which was generally the chief cause of thermal-chemical burns on most with firsthand exposure to WP. The NIF terrorists were no exception, and nearly half screamed as their clothing and flesh began to sear under the exposed chemical fragments.

Bolan peered around the corner and began picking off the terrorists who had managed to avoid the effects of the grenade. He sprayed the area with a few sustained bursts. The Executioner watched as a pair of NIF gunners managed to escape the assault and get beyond his line of sight.

Bolan knew their plan: they thought he hadn't seen them.

They would skirt the building he was using as cover and try to flank him. When they burst from the opposite end of the outbuilding, weapons at the ready, Bolan was waiting for them.

The Executioner triggered his weapon, cutting a bloody pattern across the chest and stomach of the first terrorist. The guy's intestines and lung tissue erupted from holes in his back, and he coughed a significant amount of blood before falling to the ground. His partner was no luckier as several of the high-velocity rounds caught him at the hip. Bolan finished it with a round through the falling terrorist's head.

The plane's engines were now deafening as Bolan reloaded and stepped into view. He aimed for the tires, but nearly lost his life to the sudden opening up of several more automatic weapons. A few of the NIF terrorists had apparently been instructed to stay behind and cover the escape, and it almost came to a halt right there for the warrior. Bolan managed to drop and roll away from the initial hail of bullets that either buzzed the air immediately over his head or bounced off the tarmac.

The Executioner got to one knee and let fly an angry torrent of rounds. Two terrorists were lifted off their feet by the impacts, the heavy-caliber slugs dumping them on the ground in torn, broken, bleeding heaps. Bolan caught another terrorist with a head shot, and he traded a few rounds with a fourth who managed to escape inside the building. The plane was now in position on the runway and ready for takeoff.

Bolan looked in its direction, but the sound of shooting inside the small terminal building—and subsequent panicked screams—demanded his attention. The Executioner spared one more glance at the plane before heading toward the building to dispatch the final terrorist before he could kill any more innocents.

RHATIB STARED OUT the window, watching with interest as the American headed for the charter service building. Despite the fact he loathed Americans, and everything for which they stood, he could not help but admire this man. The guy fought with the bravery and skill of a professional soldier, while simultaneously showing the determination and conviction of a demon straight from the pit of Hell. But then, there was little point in worrying about him now. Rhatib knew that it was probably the last he would ever see of the man—or of any American for that matter.

"We lost many today," Malik said, shaking his head and sighing deeply as he took the seat next to Rhatib.

"I am sorry this had to happen," Rhatib replied.

"You have no reason to be sorry. The American has been a thorn in our side. He keeps finding us, whittling away at our forces. But he does not know that we are strong. He does not know that we have hundreds—even thousands more at our disposal."

Rhatib looked at Malik, and he could not withhold an expression of regret. "Khayyat, you know that I love you like a brother, but I do not agree with you on this matter. Surely even *you* must realize that a strong army is not everything. It does not guarantee security, and it certainly does not guarantee freedom for our people from the bonds of the Americans."

"Do you not have faith in your own people?" Malik asked.

"I have faith only in certainty. And the only certainty is that we must use the precious weapons the Americans think make them so impervious against them. This is what I know and believe in, and this is what's *real* to me." He rubbed his eyes and said, "Now, I must sleep."

Sadiq Rhatib laid his head back and allowed himself to drift to another time and place; a time and place he called home.

9

Washington, D.C.

Jack Grimaldi could not recall a time he'd been happier to see the Executioner alive and well, and he didn't mind telling Bolan that. "Sarge, you are one sight for sore eyes. They made it sound as if you were near death. You don't look like hell."

"I feel like it," Bolan said, shaking Grimaldi's hand.

Stony Man's ace flier grinned good-naturedly as he stood next to the jet in his blue flight suit. Warm eyes under thick, bushy eyebrows studied MacEwan with a passive interest. His handshake was strong and warm as he clapped Bolan on the shoulder with his free hand. The Executioner had to admit he was glad to see a familiar face, too. Jack Grimaldi: Mob-pilot turned Stony Man airborne wizard. He could fly everything from a World War I twin-prop to an F-18 fighter jet, with credentials and experience that rivaled even those piloting Air Force One. Grimaldi had accompanied Bolan on thousands of missions, and dropped him into hot LZs and pulled him out of more tight scrapes around the world than either really cared to count.

"You know where we're going?" Bolan asked, once he'd assisted MacEwan up the stairwell and into the Learjet C-21A.

"Yeah. Bear is tracking them now."

Bolan nodded and without another word, Grimaldi headed for the cockpit and prepared for takeoff. The Executioner had contacted Stony Man as soon as possible and requested that Grimaldi be ready and waiting for his arrival at Dulles. They wouldn't have a lot of time, and he needed them to track the plane so they could follow it to wherever the NIF terrorists planned to go.

As Grimaldi put the plane in position and waited for take-off clearance, MacEwan turned and looked at Bolan intently. "Why don't we just blow the thing out of the sky?"

"Because I think those targets I hit at the airport were de-coys, and I'm betting that the *real* mastermind who compro-mised Carnivore's security is on that plane. We lose that, we lose our tactical advantage."

"I don't see we really have one," MacEwan replied.

"No?" Bolan said, raising his eyebrows. "If Carnivore is as complicated a system as you described, then we need this NIF hacker alive and well."

"Because otherwise is might take us years to figure out what he's done," she said.

"Exactly."

"You're assuming this person is a he?"

Bolan studied her a moment, not sure why she'd asked such a question. "What's your point?"

"Nothing, it's just that use of such a gender-specific pro-noun does indicate somewhat of a rather egocentric and ma-chismo personality."

Bolan shook his head, ready to send a biting reply her way when she suddenly cast a sideways glance at him and smiled. Okay, so she was teasing him. He could understand that, but it made him uncomfortable. This lady was one smart cookie, and she posed a unique challenge to Bolan. Not that the Executioner hadn't been around intelligent women before—certainly Barbara Price was extremely bright. There weren't many women who had a talent for using brains as a key weapon to keep a guy off balance. In the case of some of the female persuasion, it was a useless and irritating distraction to a man like Mack Bolan. In MacEwan's case, however, it was sexy.

Once they were airborne, MacEwan began to work on the signals that were still being pushed into Carnivore. She typed furiously, studied files, contrasted those files with notes from Mitchell Fowler's journal, and still she would sigh, become frustrated and beat her fist on the seat next to her.

"What's wrong?" Bolan finally asked.

"Everything's wrong," MacEwan replied in a quavery voice. "I just can't seem to figure out how they got inside Carnivore. And if I can't figure out how they got in, there's no way we can shut them out."

Grimaldi emerged from the cockpit and said, "Hey, I have a question. Why don't we just shut this Carnivore down at the source?"

MacEwan threw him a surprised look. "Who's flying the plane?"

Grimaldi jerked his thumb over his shoulder and said, "Autopilot."

"Actually, I'm forgetting my manners," Bolan said. "Tyra MacEwan, this is Jack."

"Nice to meet you Jack…?"

Grimaldi smiled and as he took her hand gently replied, "Just Jack will do, ma'am."

MacEwan noticed his unabashed stare and turned to flash Bolan a mischievous smile. "Oh, so we've got a charmer here."

"Yeah," Bolan said with a chuckle, "Jack here's real suave."

"I fly a lot," Grimaldi added. "It's a good idea to have a gal in every port."

"I'm sure," MacEwan said.

"Anyway, now that we've dispensed with the pleasantries," Bolan interjected, a cue Grimaldi should take his seat, "Jack makes a good point. Why can't we just shut Carnivore down?"

"We proposed that once, but if we do that it will be permanent. Not to mention the fact that Carnivore monitoring systems operate in thousands of different locations. Each locale has to be shut down at the source. That takes time, resources and security."

"Sheesh," Grimaldi muttered. "Tell me this isn't a government operation."

The jet shimmied just a bit, and MacEwan looked at Grimaldi with sudden concern. "Are you sure it's okay there's nobody at the wheel, Jack?"

"Just bumpy air," Grimaldi said in way of reply.

Bolan decided to jump in. "Don't worry about Jack. I wouldn't trust anybody at the stick more than him."

"It's not turbulence that bothers me," MacEwan said. "It's that other stuff like, I don't know…midair collisions."

"We're over the ocean. There's a proximity alarm set to go off if any solid object larger than a paperback comes within twenty nautical miles of this bird," Grimaldi said.

"If you say so," MacEwan replied. "Anyway, just from the logistics of it, you can see it would be a nightmare to shut off Carnivore."

"What about blocking the system electronically?" Bolan asked.

"What do mean?"

"Shut it down from the inside out," he said.

"I still don't follow."

"Well, we already know they're inside, and we can now detect them. Right? So why not trap them inside the system? Wouldn't that prevent access to other systems?"

Grimaldi laughed. "You're talking like a cockroach trap?"

"A what?" MacEwan asked.

"A cockroach trap. You know, the roaches go in, but they don't come out."

"Wait a minute, I see what you're saying," MacEwan said excitedly. "A one-way door!"

"Exactly," Bolan replied.

"Is that possible?" Grimaldi asked.

MacEwan now looked at Grimaldi like he was the pauper asking the princess for a date, although it was obvious she didn't really mean anything by it. She followed the look with a smile and a laugh. "Anything's possible, Jack. Finding a way to do it is the trick."

"Then we'd better start looking into it," Bolan said, "because it sounds like it might take some time."

"You don't know the half of it," MacEwan said. "It won't be easy on my own."

"You're not on your own," Bolan replied. "You have the unconditional support of my people, and I can tell that support comes from the highest levels. We're already confident you're on our side. I think I can trust you, and that's enough for anybody else."

MacEwan exchanged glances with Bolan and then Grimaldi, who nodded as if to say it was the absolute truth and she should believe it. MacEwan still looked skeptical, but she had already committed herself to trusting Bolan, and the Executioner knew she wouldn't let them down. If there was anything he'd learned about this tough and intelligent woman in the past twenty-four hours, it was that once she had committed to something, she stuck with it to the bitter end.

"Then I guess I'll just have to find a way to stop this maniac," she said, nodding.

"There's a lot at stake," Bolan said.

"Don't remind me," MacEwan said as she cracked her knuckles and got to work.

"Well, guess I better get back to my business," Grimaldi said. As he started for the cockpit, he stopped himself and looked back at MacEwan, who was now engrossed with the computer.

"Hey, lady."

She looked up from her notebook.

"Do you *really* think you can do all that crap you just said?"

MacEwan grinned. "I don't know. Do you think you can put this bird down in one piece?"

"Ha!" Grimaldi replied, turning and muttering, "Child's play."

Once Grimaldi was gone, and some time of silence had elapsed between them, MacEwan turned to Bolan. He noticed her staring at him, and he returned her stare. He could see a slight waver in her confidence, but he wasn't going to say anything about it. He knew she'd come through, one way or another. His main task would be to keep her alive long enough to finish the job.

"You have something else you want to tell me?" he asked.

"Even if this is possible, Cooper," MacEwan retorted, "I'm concerned it won't do us much good. I can only stop further communications, but I can't undo what's been done. In order to trap this hacker *inside* the system, I have to find the entry point. Then I have to find a way to turn that into our one-way door."

"Then I'd get to work," Bolan replied with a reassuring smile. "I have a feeling we're not going anywhere for a while."

And with that, the pair went about their own special tasks, her finding a way to trap the NIF inside Carnivore, him preparing his equipment for another bloody encounter.

An encounter Mack Bolan knew was inevitable.

RHATIB SMILED with satisfaction as he watched the tracking system tracing his phantom signals throughout Carnivore. It would take them some time to determine they led nowhere, and by that time he'd have complete control.

What bothered him most was the interference coming from a rogue network that he couldn't identify. All of the IP numbers were blocked, and there were intrusion detection systems, self-destruct scripts and firewall configurations—both at the hardware and software level—that were so complex he was having trouble accessing them. It seemed like Carnivore, the great watcher, had a watcher of its own. There was some system monitoring Carnivore, generating one of the strongest signals he'd ever seen.

Cracking into Carnivore security had actually been child's play for Rhatib. It was amazing how far a little cash would go. He paid some computer hardware geeks to place some innocent-looking little devices inside the major hubs in Boston, Denver and Los Angeles. With that, he was inside the network and able to actually feed off the signals in those Carnivore servers. That, in turn, had allowed him electronic access into the rest of them, and then it was just a matter of time before he had cracked all of the security codes.

His first target was the American intelligence network. Once he was into Carnivore, Rhatib had pulled every possible bit of documented information he could off the system, including where additional paper files were available. The NIF then solicited in-country members in high-ranking positions, or those members of the military and civilian branches with sufficient security clearance, to make copies of the most sensitive of electronic information.

Members who didn't cooperate had either been bribed or blackmailed, depending who and where. Any who were violently opposed were killed immediately, and their deaths were all made to look like random criminal acts so the police were not suspicious. Eventually, Rhatib had enough information to carry the process forward. Within less than two years he had control and knowledge of the electronic and logistics network of nearly every intelligence agency in the American arsenal.

His next target was U.S. defense systems. He needed control over American air-to-surface missile grids and movement of naval forces. The combined bombings of the marine and naval amphibious forces had practically devastated his country, and he intended to insure that it didn't happen again. The next time the Americans fired on Afghanistan, by air or land, they would end up destroying their own. Rhatib intended to make sure of this.

Meanwhile, he had to deal with the mysterious network and devise a plan to counteract the foolish attempts by the American woman working for DARPA to track him.

The phantom signals wouldn't work forever, but they

would buy him some time. The only thing he had to avoid was getting trapped inside the system; such a possibility existed, and it was always a danger. For the moment, he was able to enter and exit through the same portal, but if they shut it as an exit point using some type of code, it would take precious time to break it.

"You look upset," Malik said to his youthful charge. "Is there something I can do?"

Although he couldn't explain why, Rhatib was irritated at first, but he quickly let the feeling pass. Malik didn't understand. Rhatib could not bring himself to yell at his friend, although the urge had struck him. Malik was only trying to help. He wasn't a stupid man by any measure, but he didn't understand a thing about technology. He thought most problems could be solved with a threat, and if that didn't work then he would employ other, more physical methods of getting the job done. It was an admirable trait for a man in his position, but it was wholly ineffective in a situation like the present one.

Rhatib was blessed with the ability to think in the abstract. He was also intuitive, something his school professors had noticed immediately about him. He was able to produce results on anything to which he put his mind. He could calculate complex equations in his head within seconds; write near-perfect software programs and code effortlessly, and in a matter of minutes resolve system problems that would otherwise have taken a cybernetics team hours or possibly days to fix.

For Rhatib, his talents were simultaneously a blessing and a curse. He loved the daily challenges, but he hated always having to use his talents for the betterment of the NIF cause. After all, he had his own agenda and while he was more than intelligent enough to devise a scheme that would accomplish both his objectives, and those of his benefactors, he was not a patient man. It was a character flaw, but also a part of his personality. He just wanted to do what he needed to get the job accomplished, but his uncle had insisted he coordinate his efforts with those of the NIF's supporters inside America. It always seemed like he was ready to implement the next stage of the plan, but the rest of them were just lagging behind.

"I appreciate your offer, my friend," Rhatib said, "but this is my work and I must do it. May I tell you something personal?"

Malik shrugged and grinned a partially toothless grin. "Of course."

"It's this waiting for our friends in America that gets to me most." Rhatib shook his head and clucked his tongue. "It seems as if we're *always* waiting for them to meet their end of the bargain. This constant delay is inefficient, and you know I cannot stand inefficiency."

"I understand, Sadiq, but we have no choice. Your uncle was very clear that we must cooperate with men like this Lenzini, and—"

"I don't trust Lenzini," Rhatib said. He spit on the floor. "He's a filthy dog, just like the rest of his kind."

"I do not trust him either, but our orders are clear."

"Orders from whom? My uncle?" Rhatib waved dismissively. "My uncle doesn't understand the situation. It is critical we accomplish all tasks in the next forty-eight hours. Otherwise we risk exposure and failure. These American criminals and their inept friends are holding us back. I *must* be allowed to proceed very soon or all will be lost."

"Then I would think we must begin applying pressure in areas we had not previously considered critical," Malik said. "What do you propose?"

GET FREE BOOKS and a FREE GIFT
WHEN YOU PLAY THE...

7 Lucky

SLOT MACHINE GAME!

Just scratch off the silver box with a coin. Then check below to see the gifts you get!

YES! I have scratched off the silver box. Please send me the 2 free Gold Eagle® books and gift for which I qualify. I understand I am under no obligation to purchase any books, as explained on the back of this card.

366 ADL D34F   **166 ADL D34E**

FIRST NAME

LAST NAME

ADDRESS

APT.#

CITY

STATE/PROV.

ZIP/POSTAL CODE

7	7	7	**Worth TWO FREE BOOKS plus a BONUS Mystery Gift!**
🍒	🍒	🍒	**Worth TWO FREE BOOKS!**
♣	♣	♣	**Worth ONE FREE BOOK!**
🔔	🔔	🍒	**TRY AGAIN!**

(MB-04-R)

DETACH AND MAIL CARD TODAY!

The Gold Eagle Reader Service™ — Here's how it works:

Accepting your 2 free books and mystery gift places you under no obligation to buy anything. You may keep the books and gift and return the shipping statement marked "cancel." If you do not cancel, about a month later we'll send you 6 additional books and bill you just $29.94* — that's a saving of over 10% off the cover price of all 6 books! And there's no extra charge for shipping! You may cancel at any time, but if you choose to continue, every other month we'll send you 6 more books, which you may either purchase at the discount price or return to us and cancel your subscription.

*Terms and prices subject to change without notice. Sales tax applicable in N.Y. Canadian residents will be charged applicable provincial taxes and GST. Credit or debit balances in a customer's account(s) may be offset by any other outstanding balance owed by or to the customer.

"Well, we are confident that this American with whom we fought in Washington will follow us."

"I am counting on this."

"He probably knows that you are, if he is as clever as I first suspected. I think he has very powerful friends," Malik replied.

"Perhaps his friends are behind this anonymous network," Rhatib interjected. "I am going to see if I can crack their security. In the meantime, you have a plan?"

"Now that Fowler is dead, the DARPA woman remains the only one who has a sense for what is happening. I suspect that the American will need her support. He will surely keep her close."

"You believe that if we maximize our efforts in destroying her, that it will stop him from ruining our plans?" Rhatib was smiling.

"I don't know that with any certainty," Malik replied. "But it seems our best option. What I cannot risk is losing the support of my men because I do not take revenge on this American for killing so many of our people in Washington."

"He is a very dangerous and methodical man," Rhatib said, nodding in agreement. He lowered his voice and added, "You cannot let him castrate you in front of your men. This would bring shame to your ancestors."

Rhatib could see his comment stung Malik, and there was a reddening hue to his face that was partially embarrassment, partially anger. "I meant no offense to you, my friend. Please accept by apologies. I was just trying to make a point," he said.

"And you have made it," Malik said quietly. "I will take care of this American. You have the most secure methods of communication. Contact our men and let them know to prepare for his arrival. We will teach this American once and for all that this is our war, and that nothing can stand in our way. He is one man, and this is jihad."

Malik's last words dripped with bitter resentment and revenge. "The American will pay for his interference. He will pay with his life. I swear it."

10

Afghanistan

Colonel Umar Abdalrahman sat in his cold, cramped office and waited anxiously for news that Rhatib had arrived safely in the country.

According to Abdalrahman's superiors, the plan was supposed to have been simple. Penetrate the American electronics defense systems using the FBI's packet snooper, Carnivore, as the communications pathway. While it sounded simple, that wasn't quite all there was to it. It had taken them many months to set it up. Were it not for the technical genius of Rhatib, they probably wouldn't have made it this far.

Sadiq Rhatib was Abdalrahman's only living relative besides his wife, and he loved that boy dearly. After his brother was lost defending Afghanistan against the alleged "freedom fighters" in the north, they were forced into hiding in the mountains. Abdalrahman swore he would defend his nation and preserve the life of his nephew to his dying breath. The enemy murdered Afghan women and children, assisted by an army of American infidels. They had pillaged and raped a great land, and destroyed the Taliban. Abdalrahman watched the American television news while U.S. armed forces bombed holes in his beautiful country, and then the gutless soldiers in the north followed and decimated everything left in the wake of the bombings.

It showed their spineless ways, and it demonstrated that there wasn't one member outside of the original group dedicated to the cause of al Qaeda who could be trusted. Even some of those within the group had betrayed the cause and the trust of the Taliban. There seemed this total lack of control and discipline on the part of some members once they got outside the sphere and influence of the fatwahs. Those declarations of war against the Americans were the fabric that held their brotherhood together, and Abdalrahman meant to keep it together.

It was all for the greater glory of Allah and the security of His nation.

The satellite telephone rang and shook Abdalrahman from his daydreaming. He snatched the oversized receiver as he cursed himself for succumbing to the thoughts of glory and victory. He was a serious soldier and a religious man. If he did not tolerate such activities from his men, he certainly could not tolerate them in himself.

"Yes?" he barked into the phone.

"We have received a message, sir."

Abdalrahman didn't have to ask from whom the message originated. Even through the crackling static he recognized the voice of his contact in Peshawar.

"Are they close?" he asked the caller.

"Yes, Colonel," the man replied. "They have advised that Americans are following them."

"Take care of it," Abdalrahman replied. "Understood?"

"Understood, sir."

Abdalrahman disconnected the call, then sat back in his chair and rubbed his eyes. He could not believe that Malik had allowed the Americans to follow them this far. He would have to give that man a good tongue-lashing when he returned. Of course, he would do it in the right place and the right time, without Rhatib or any of Malik's other men present. This was something between Abdalrahman and Malik, and not for the ears of anyone else.

In the meantime, his men would deal with whoever was pursuing them; Abdalrahman had no concerns about that. They would deal swiftly and mercilessly with their enemies, and they would show no restraint, as they'd had to in America. These fools had followed his people with callous disregard for their own safety. They were dangerous, and Abdalrahman knew not to underestimate his enemies. Still, all he could do was wait for them to arrive.

And if anything happened to Rhatib, the Americans would pay.

PAKISTAN HAD ALWAYS played an important role in the political and military history of the world, and Peshawar—capital of the North West Frontier Province—had shared in that heritage. Peshawar blended the old with the new in a unique way. It was divided into three major sections, one of which—known as *cantonment*—was the most commercialized and modern area of the three. The other two comprised a residential area and a historical area referred to by most tourists as the "old town."

Despite the stereotypes placed upon many of the nationalities and religious sects of the Middle East, Mack Bolan knew the majority of Islamists were peaceful people who just wanted to live their lives without worrying about the threat of constant bloodshed and conflict. Hatred of Americans was an ideology only a small percentage of Middle Eastern people supported, but unfortunately it was promoted through the political machines of many governments. The only way those dictators and political extremists could survive in office was by oppressing their people and then blaming that oppression on Western cultures and religious principles.

Nonetheless, Pakistan was on friendly terms with the United States, so Bolan didn't expect much trouble from the authorities. In fact, they didn't really have time to give him any trouble, since the approaching group of men, which Bolan immediately marked as a terrorist hit team, signaled there would be enough trouble for both him and the customs officer now managing the line of people in which Bolan stood. While Peshawar International Airport wasn't exactly a study in hustle and bustle, there were still enough innocents around that Bolan knew he had only two choices: take out the terrorists quickly or take the fight somewhere else.

Bolan decided on the latter.

On seeing their approach, the Executioner turned and walked briskly back in the direction of the small hangar Grimaldi had secured with a smile and a thousand dollars in U.S. cash. As Bolan walked, he checked behind him to make sure the terrorists were following him—they were. As inconspicuously as possible, he reached beneath his jacket and withdrew the Beretta 93-R, turned the selector to 3-round-burst mode and thumbed the safety.

The group had now passed the customs police, who were watching Bolan with suspicion, wondering why he had suddenly left his bag of clothes sitting at the table. One of the of-

ficers recognized the fact that trouble was brewing because he shouted at the group of men. The terrorists ignored the officer, and when he started to step forward in pursuit and shouted at them again, one of the men produced a machine pistol and started to turn in the officer's direction.

Bolan realized the customs officer was going to die if he didn't act immediately. His line of fire was clear. The warrior turned suddenly, snap-aimed the Beretta and smoothly squeezed the trigger. The Executioner had loaded the Beretta for bear this time, substituting the usual low-grain, subsonic loads with 158-grain hardballs. All three steel-jacketed slugs caught the terrorist gunner in the back before he could shoot the customs officer.

Bolan went into a shoulder roll as soon as the shots were away. Years of combat experience had taught him that a soldier was most vulnerable right after pulling the trigger, since he wasn't physically able to take up both an offensive and defensive posture simultaneously. That meant he had to switch from one to the other, and he had to be able to do it damn quick. Bolan was one of those few who could not only understand the principle, but could also put it into motion with marked effectiveness.

The rest of the terrorists had now exposed their weapons, but Bolan had accomplished his mission in the sense that no innocents were in the line of fire.

Even as the terrorist bullets zinged off the floor and walls, the Executioner rolled to a kneeling position and acquired his next target. Excluding the one he'd brought down, there were still four to deal with. Bolan took the next gunman with a perfect 3-shot grouping in the upper body, one of the rounds ripping through the man's neck. The terrorist did an odd flip as the 9 mm slugs struck him, and his body collapsed on the floor.

There was the sound of a series of shots coming from a semiauto pistol, and Bolan turned to see that Jack Grimaldi had grabbed cover and was now dealing out some of his own justice. Stony Man's ace pilot popped off several bursts from a .45-caliber version of the H&K P-9. Several of the rounds hit home, punching through the face of one of the terrorists.

Bolan tracked one NIF gunman moving away from his comrades. The guy was obviously trying to flank their position, but the Executioner knew that trick. He steadied his aim and squeezed the trigger, as the customs officers—pistols now drawn—opened fire at the same time. The running terrorist fell under a hail of semiauto pistol rounds, caught in a merciless cross fire that ripped holes in his tender flesh. He staggered in place a moment, almost as if he didn't know which way to fall, before finally collapsing prone on the floor.

The last terrorist dropped his weapon and charged Bolan and Grimaldi, screaming at the top of his lungs as he closed the gap. The duo opened up simultaneously, but the forward motion of the man—combined with an obvious surge of adrenaline—got him close enough to make his intentions obvious. Even as the first of Grimaldi's and Bolan's rounds struck him, the terrorist still had enough time to expose the high explosives strapped to his body. Bolan shouted a warning as he got to his feet and rushed Grimaldi's position. He reached out and practically clotheslined the pilot as he brought both of them to the ground. There was an abrupt flash of light as the terrorist ignited the HE, blowing his body to kingdom come. White-hot flames and debris flew over their heads, and their bodies were pelted by the falling rain of destructive elements, but they were far enough from the blast to avoid any real injury.

"You okay?" Bolan asked as he rose and then assisted Grimaldi to his feet.

"Yeah," the pilot replied. "Thanks, Sarge. I owe you—"

"Nothing," the soldier finished for him.

Grimaldi grasped Bolan's shoulder and nodded with a grin. A fresh band of shots rang out, and the pair turned to see approaching customs officers, their pistol muzzles winking.

"Uh-oh," Grimaldi said. "Looks like we've worn out our welcome."

"Let's go!" Bolan commanded.

The two turned and left the terminal the way they came. They sprinted across the tarmac, heading in the direction of the hangar. A shout drew their attention, and they turned to see MacEwan yanking a small, lanky baggage handler from his idling vehicle.

"What the hell is she doing?" Grimaldi asked.

As Bolan changed direction and headed for MacEwan, who was now climbing behind the wheel he replied, "I thought she was going to stay in the plane?"

"She was supposed to!" Grimaldi snapped as he struggled to keep up with the Executioner's long, powerful strides.

"Going my way, boys?" MacEwan asked when they were in earshot.

"Drive!" Bolan commanded as he and Grimaldi piled into the other side.

The baggage vehicle lurched as MacEwan tromped on the pedal. Anybody in half-decent shape would be able to outrun the antiquated car, since it didn't go all that fast, and had a dead man's brake to boot. Still, Bolan figured when the customs officers cleared the terminal they would be looking for two escapees on foot, and paying little attention to ground equipment activity. It might buy them some time.

"What did you think you were doing?" Grimaldi asked MacEwan, pounding his fist on the dash.

MacEwan's dark hair danced in the icy breeze whistling through the open-air cab as she replied, "A deaf person could have heard that commotion. Sounded like you had trouble so I figured we'd need some wheels."

"Another stunt like that and I'll tie you up for the remainder of this little expedition," Bolan replied with a look as cold as the air. "You understand?"

"I understand."

When they'd reached the perimeter of the airport, Bolan ordered them to abandon the baggage truck, then ignited the thing with an incendiary grenade.

"Giving us some extra time to split?" Grimaldi asked with a grin.

Bolan nodded. "Eventually, you'll have to get back to the plane. Right now, I don't think the Peshawar authorities have any way to tie us to it, so it should stay secure. We'll have to work out a plan later to get you back there."

"The guy I paid promised to keep his mouth shut if anyone did come poking around," Grimaldi replied.

"Good."

Bolan turned and clipped away enough of the fence to get them on the other side of airport property.

"What now?" MacEwan asked as the Executioner led them into an easy trot across a field.

"We'll be able to lose ourselves in those woods up ahead," Bolan said. "I remember our maps showed a highway on the other side of them. We should be able to get a lift to a phone."

"Then what?"

"Then I take care of business," the Executioner replied.

WITHIN AN HOUR of calling Stony Man, the weary trio found themselves secure in a mortar and sandstone hovel situated in the old town. The place was dusty, mite infested and reeked of a combination of scents none of them would even have cared to guess on, but it was safe and quiet, and that was enough for now.

All three of them eagerly consumed their *chappli kebabs*—a traditional favorite consisting of spicy beef mixed with eggs, corn flour, green chilies and tomatoes served on unleavened bread—while under the watchful eye of their host, Musa al-Dawud. The water wasn't the best, but their host had assured them it was potable, evidenced by the metallic smell of iodine wafting from it, and the nearly chlorinelike aftertaste that struck the senses almost immediately after the first swallow.

Al-Dawud sat peacefully in the corner, chewing on his pipe and occasionally taking a sip from a dirty china cup filled with dark-leaf green tea. He didn't say much, apparently content to observe his visitors rather than interrupt their meal with a lot of idle chitchat. Bolan could appreciate the man's introspective nature, but he could also tell that al-Dawud was full of curiosity about them. After all, the man was risking his hide to stow three fugitives who would otherwise be holed up in some dark and dank Peshawar jail. Bolan figured he owed the old man an explanation, even if the information was minimal.

"You're wondering about our intent here."

The man pulled the pipe from his mouth, exhaled a cloud of smoke and said, "I do not wonder."

"Come on," Grimaldi said with a cocksure grin around a

mouthful of half-chewed food. "You're not even the least bit interested in why we're here?"

"He does not care," a soft, clear voice replied behind them. The trio turned to see that a dark-skinned, petite woman had entered the house and, in all likelihood, had been watching them for some time.

"Who are you?" Bolan asked.

She smiled. "I am the one who arranged to hide you here."

"You mean *you're* their contact?" MacEwan asked with a surprised expression.

"Does this shock you?" she said as she walked around the cracked, wooden pallets covered by a thin mattress on which they were sitting while they ate.

The woman folded her legs under her and sat down with the grace and balance of a ballerina. She did not appear to be of Arab ancestry, and Bolan immediately noted this about her, along with her striking beauty. Her black hair was straight and shiny, and extended to her waist. The deeply set eyes were like black marbles, brilliant even under the dim lantern light, and the face—thin but not gaunt—was sculptured with high cheekbones and sensuous but determined lips. Dark, full eyebrows only enhanced her almost picturesque beauty.

"What's your name?" Grimaldi asked.

In singsong but very clear English, she replied, "My real name would most likely be unpronounceable to you, so if you wish you may call me Saura."

"You're Indian," Bolan observed.

"Yes."

"That's amazing," MacEwan interjected. "An Indian in Pakistan?"

"Not everyone in my country is at war with Pakistan," she

replied. "Like you, miss, I am a well-educated woman. And as such, I have come to understand that not everyone believes in the political ideologies of terrorists or puppet governments. This is why I am here. I am here to help keep peace between our peoples."

"But these people have caused you great suffering."

"Look around you," she said, making an encompassing gesture of the room and looking toward the ceiling. She paused for effect and then looked MacEwan in the eye and continued, "There is great suffering everywhere. I did not come here to solve all of the world's problems. I came to ease whatever pain I could."

"How so?" MacEwan asked, fascinated.

"I am a doctor," she replied. "As you can see, the people in this part of the city are not exactly in the best health. Disease runs rampant here. Unchecked. Many suffer and few do anything to alleviate that suffering. I decided to do something."

"Why are you helping us then?" Bolan asked in a quiet, gentle voice.

Saura looked at him with an expression that seemed almost like curiosity combined with amusement. "Because I know you are here for the same reason I am, Mr. Cooper. You are here to end the suffering."

The Executioner would never have admitted to anyone else that her answer surprised him, but he realized in that brief moment—a moment that seemed like a suspension of time and space—he was looking at a woman who truly understood him.

At first, Bolan had struggled with the everlasting death and destruction of his war against the Mafia. But as he'd continued on, and eventually reached further to fight a war against international terrorism, Bolan had come full circle and re-signed himself to a duty few others could or would perform. He knew that through all of the suffering, and all of the lives he'd been forced to take in order to save the lives of millions more, that there was something fundamentally right about his war.

Now a woman sat in front of him who seemed to understand that as well.

Saura gestured to al-Dawud. "These are my friends. Musa is a local doctor to these people, although you would probably call him more of a medicine man. Still, he managed to get me into this country so I could help these people."

She turned to look at Bolan again and said, "So in return, I help people like you. Even though I know what you're here to do—as do my friends—we understand that the suffering must stop if we are ever to mature as a world population."

"You know, everything you're saying and doing sure sounds admirable," Grimaldi said. "But, lady, I'm here to tell you that I don't think the human race will ever reach the point where we can just get along with each other."

"You'll have to forgive him," MacEwan said, jerking her thumb in Grimaldi's direction. "He's an eternal pessimist. I think what you're doing here is incredible."

Bolan finally said, "Look, I think we understand each other, and I also admire what you're doing. But the fact of the matter is that the longer we wait, the less our chances of finding the last of these NIF terrorists. We need a way to track them down, and this place just isn't going to cut it."

"What is it that you think you need, Mr. Cooper?" Saura asked.

"Well, I'm going to need weapons."

"That is not a problem," she said with a shrug.

"Really? How about electricity and a phone?" He gestured to MacEwan and added, "This woman holds the only key to locating the bad guys, and I don't even know how we can get her equipment from our plane."

"I will take care of it," al-Dawud said.

"And I will help you procure firearms," Saura added. "Will there be anything else?"

"That should cover it," Bolan replied. "When the time comes, I'll do the rest."

11

If there was any place in all of Pakistan to find guns, it was the village of Zarghun Khel. The place had been manufacturing everything from cheap knockoffs to quality replicas of guns from all over the world for more than a century, and the village was, even in the most literal sense, a one-stop gun factory along what was known as the Tribal Belt. Nearly every tradesman in every village home was a gunsmith, each one varying in degrees of specialty and skill.

Saura recommended a gunsmith by name, and arranged for them to embark on the forty-some kilometer trip the next morning aboard a very dilapidated Land Rover. Travel to Zarghun Khel was forbidden without a permit from the Pakistani Secretariat, but Saura seemed to already have those documents. The military troops guarding the entry areas of the village hardly gave them a second glance as she showed them the permit and forged medical credentials she'd procured for Bolan.

"What is the purpose of your visit?" the guard asked.

"Medical checkups of village members, sir," Saura answered, smiling sweetly at her interrogator.

The Pakistani officer eyed Bolan with a bit more scrutiny and suspicion than he did Saura, but soon they were past the double checkpoints and rolling into the village. Bolan was impressed by the woman seated next to him. She seemed so fragile and delicate in that petite frame, yet she had a heart as large as the sun, and a tough mental attitude that would have put some U.S. Navy SEALs to shame.

The sound of gunfire caused the Executioner to drop his hand to the butt of the Beretta tucked beneath the ratty, two-sizes-too-small woolen overcoat al-Dawud had loaned him.

"It is okay," Saura said. "Just buyers testing the merchandise."

Bolan eased up and said, "Fine. But I get real nervous around guns where I'm not the one with my finger on the trigger."

"You must know this is actually a way of life for many of these people. It is possible that they know more about firearms than even you, Mr. Cooper."

"You think so?" Bolan quipped.

"It would not surprise me if it were so."

Yeah, Saura was a hell of a lady, that was for sure. A guy like Bolan couldn't help but admire her.

"So just how do you plan to pay for this?" Bolan asked.

"I don't."

"You want to explain that?"

"Not really." She spared him a glance before looking at the backbreaking main road passing through the village, and added, "Is it not simply enough that I know someone who can help you with what you need?"

"It's enough," Bolan said. "I just like to know what I'm walking into."

"Why is this so important to you?"

"Just addicted to staying alive," he replied with a shrug. "I'm kind of funny like that."

"You do not trust so easily, I think, Mr. Cooper."

"You know, why don't you just call me Matt."

She nodded as she began to brake and then turned suddenly into an alleyway between two of the traditional mud and brick homes. Most of the residences within the village wouldn't have passed even the most lax building codes in American slums, but here it was simply everyday life. Nobody gave a thought or a damn if one house was a little nicer than another, or if a neighbor seemed to be getting along better. Villagers in areas like these were like family, and they shared a lot with one another. That spirit of cooperation is what probably kept them alive in a country that had always endured war and poverty in one fashion or another.

At the end of the alley was a boxy structure with some sort of blanket draped along its front. It seemed to Bolan that Saura wasn't going to stop the Land Rover, and it surprised him when she drove right through the canvaslike material and into the darkened shelter. She braked suddenly and killed the engine, and Bolan had to wait a moment for his eyes to adjust. The crude enclosure obviously served as a sort of makeshift garage. Its walls were lined with a variety of auto mechanic's tools.

"Please come with me," Saura said.

Bolan followed her as they walked through a narrow doorway leading from the garage to an even darker enclosure. They descended a sharp stairwell and soon found themselves in a dimly lit basement with a ceiling that was so low Bolan had to hunch in order to keep from smacking his head.

The room into which the stairwell emerged wasn't that big, maybe ten-by-ten feet, with a simple cot and an old, portable black-and-white television that was hooked up to a car battery. Bolan could hardly believe the thing was capable of working, let alone receiving a signal. Still, he decided to reserve judgment until he'd actually met his benefactor.

He didn't have to wait long. The room adjoined with another one, connected by a doorway almost identical to the one leading from the garage to the stairwell. Sharp, familiar scents immediately assaulted his nostrils, and Bolan recognized the odors of gun oils, nitro solvents, machined parts and freshly stained wood. Even under the dim lights, there was no mistaking the gleaming blued finishes of automatic rifles and machine pistols stacked neatly in racks affixed to the walls.

The center of the small shop was taken up by a variety of wood and metal machining tools; they were very expensive tools and extremely high quality, which meant they were probably used to produce firearms of the same caliber. Bolan couldn't help but be impressed. However, his surprise at the quality workmanship of the hardware didn't come anywhere close to the shock he experienced at laying eyes on the master behind such craftsmanship. Near one of the benches, a little man with a long gray beard sat hunkered over the L-frame of a revolver. He didn't notice them at all, apparently fixated on his work with an expression that seemed as carefree and loving as that of a mother changing her child's diaper.

"Hello again, Bashar," Saura said.

The old man looked up slowly, and the expression became one of recognition—friendly recognition. The man groaned earnestly, rose from his stool and rushed toward them with arms wide open. Saura hugged the old man without any hesitation, and when they finally parted she reached into her coat and withdrew a wadded paper bag.

Bolan stood quietly, watching the exchange, keeping his eyes focused on the crinkled roll of paper Saura handed to Bashar. She turned and noticed he was staring, and she smiled and shook her head.

"Always so suspicious, Matt." She leaned close to him and whispered, "It's medicine. He's sick with bone cancer."

Bolan nodded and relaxed. Why the hell was he so jumpy? He thought he could trust Saura, and he didn't see how this old man could pose a threat, but something still bothered him. Things had gone like clockwork since his arrival, except for the airport encounter, and the Executioner had learned long ago that when things were consistently going well, it was never a good idea to bank on them staying that way. Reality just dictated otherwise, and Bolan had always learned to trust his instincts when it came to things like this.

Saura returned her attention to the old man and began to speak to him in Punjabi. Bolan wasn't all that comfortable with the exchange, but he knew it was necessary since the old man probably didn't speak one bit of English. After several minutes, Saura turned to him and smiled.

"He wants to know what you need."

Bolan gestured toward the racks and looked expectantly at the old man. He flashed Saura a suspicious look, but when she nodded and smiled he gestured for Bolan to help himself. The Executioner began walking the racks. Within a minute, he'd picked out a variant but almost exact replica of an Israeli-made Galil.

Bolan also spotted a new weapon that he'd test-fired a couple of times before, but was surprised to see it in the basement workshop of an aged Pakistani gunsmith. The weapon was an automatic shotgun developed jointly between U.S. and German gun engineers. The CAWS—close-assault-weapon system—was tough and lightweight. A 10-round box magazine fed 76 mm 12-gauge shotgun shells containing eight tungsten alloy pellets that could penetrate body armor-grade steel up to 150 meters. With a cyclic rate of 200 rounds per minute, the CAWS was as pure a fighting tool as any other Bolan had used before.

He indicated the two weapons, and the old man nodded with an almost contemplative expression before turning to Saura and speaking rapidly to her in his native tongue. Bashar then turned back to Bolan, winked at him with an ingratiating smile and went to one of the many cupboards built into the wall beneath the racks.

"He says you have excellent tastes," Saura told Bolan.

The Executioner nodded while keeping one eye on the old man. The earlier sense of some impending danger, that gnawing of distrust, was starting to recede. It looked like Saura had some sort of deal worked out with the old man. Maybe she'd traded the medicine for the guns. Whatever the case, he didn't much care as long as he could get what he needed and get out of the village with it.

Bashar produced a couple of ammunition cans for Bolan's inspection, and the Executioner found preloaded magazines for both the Galil and the CAWS. Additionally, he noticed that there were four extra boxes of ammo, two each of 9 mm semi-jacketed hollowpoints and .44 Magnum shells. Bolan looked at the man expectantly, but Bashar just kept grinning from ear to ear.

"Your pilot friend told me you would be needing extra for the guns you were able to get into Pakistan," Saura said. "I passed that information onto Bashar here."

Bolan nodded at Bashar with respect. The old man sure did know his business. The soldier reached into his pocket and withdrew a wad of cash. He peeled five Ben Franklins from the stack and handed them to Bashar, but the old man seemed hesitant to take the money.

"Saura, tell him to take it. It will keep him in food and medicine for quite awhile," Bolan said.

Saura repeated Bolan's message and the old man finally agreed, taking the money gingerly and stuffing it into some hidden area beneath his robes. Bolan grabbed the two weapons, tucking one under each arm, then snatched the ammunition cans and headed for the exit. The numbers were ticking down and he knew it wouldn't be too much longer before all hope of finding the NIF terrorists would be lost.

"We're out of time," he told Saura. "Let's go."

MacEwan and Grimaldi picked their way past the crowded vendor stalls and throngs of shoppers crammed into the old central square of Peshawar. Even in the early-morning chill, the place was packed with a line of money changers squatting on carpets who were ready to cash any form of currency— provided it was in large denominations. It was amusing to Grimaldi that in such a traditional setting as this the vendors lining the streets with their carts of crafts and handmade pottery had ultra-modern safes in which they kept their money. And when they weren't peddling to the passersby or tourists, they sat beneath umbrellas wearing brand-name American sunglasses and chatting endlessly on cellular phones.

Grimaldi had been in nearly every country in the world since joining the Stony Man team, and he'd seen many strange things in that time. So it didn't surprise him to see the influence—the *Western* influence—modern technology had on even the most traditional societies. It just plain amused him.

"Why are you smirking?" MacEwan asked him.

"Was I?" Grimaldi played dumb.

"Yes," MacEwan said, narrowing her eyes and looking at him with mock suspicion. She raised one of her lovely eyebrows and added, "What's so funny?"

Grimaldi almost didn't feel like explaining it, but he decided what the hell and told her what was on his mind.

"Yeah," she said when he'd finished his explanation. "That is pretty funny."

They walked a little longer before Grimaldi said, "I don't know why we couldn't go to the airport with Musa. It makes me damned nervous having to walk around here and act like some buggy-eyed tourist while we wait on others." He smacked his fist into his palm and added, "I want some action."

"Be careful what you wish for," MacEwan said, wagging her finger at him. She reached into the bag of dates she'd bought and popped one in her mouth. When she'd chewed it sufficiently, she continued, "Although I have to admit, that little escape we pulled off yesterday was kind of fun."

Grimaldi grunted. "Easy for you to say, lady. Nobody was shooting at you."

She nodded. "Yeah, I guess I just missed out on the best stuff. Say, can I ask you a question?"

"Shoot."

"How long have you known Cooper?"

Grimaldi felt a twinge in his gut. Something in the question set off all kinds of warning bells at first, but he thought it through quickly. The Stony Man pilot realized that MacEwan didn't really know anybody, and she'd decided to put her hands in the lives of complete strangers. She was in a foreign country with people she didn't know, on the run for her life, and pretty much at the mercy of them to figure out what the hell was going on. She was just like the other members of Stony Man in a lot of respects; an ordinary woman placed in extraordinary circumstances. She was reaching out, and Grimaldi saw no reason to slap her down for it.

"A *very* long time," he replied. "Naturally, that's about all I can say on the matter."

"I can understand that. I'm not a complete idiot."

Grimaldi stopped and touched her arm in a firm but gentle way. "I think you're anything but stupid, Tyra. Matter of fact, I'd box the ears off anyone who said you were an idiot. You may prove to be the one person who can help us defeat the NIF."

She smiled at him and then reached up and, to Grimaldi's complete surprise, planted a peck on his cheek. "Thanks, Jack. It's nice of you to say that. I wish Cooper felt that way."

Grimaldi turned and they continued walking through the market. "He does. He just has a tough time showing it. Matt's a guy of few words. He's more the kind of guy who believes that actions speak louder than words." The pilot chuckled, then added, "And believe me, he shouts."

"He's a hard man to understand."

"Yeah," Grimaldi said quietly. "Seems like I've known him all my life, and I still have trouble figuring him out sometimes."

"Mysterious and complicated?"

Grimaldi didn't even have to think about his answer. "Mysterious—no. Complicated—hell, yeah. Most complicated guy I know. And still he always does what's right, regardless of any costs to him personally. He believes in fighting for those who can't fight for themselves, and *that's* what makes him who he is."

MacEwan shook her head. "That's one heck of a life to live."

"Yeah." He looked at her and asked, "What about you? How did you get into the area of defense technology?"

"Just lucky, I guess," she said. "I started off with an interest in computers when I was in high school, although they hadn't advanced all that much. First computer I ever used belonged to my father. I remember how he said never to touch it, but I was a kid and naturally curious. Before long, I knew more about that thing than anybody in my family."

Grimaldi could see something distant and far away in MacEwan's eyes. God, she was a beautiful gal. In another place and time, Grimaldi might have made his move, but he had to be sensible. He believed there was a place and time for everything, and this was neither the place nor time for romance.

"I imagine you know quite a bit about computers, being a pilot and all," MacEwan said.

Grimaldi nodded. "That's for sure. I keep up on the latest technologies in the aerospace industry. Have to in today's world, or you get left behind. Of course, my knowledge is probably much more limited than yours."

"Where did you learn to—?" she started to ask, but then stopped short and said, "Oh, sorry. Guess you can't tell me that."

"It's okay," he said with a disarming grin. "There's nothing secret about that—"

Grimaldi's lightning-fast reflexes kicked in as four caftan-wearing men came out of nowhere. Had Grimaldi not seen the flash of sunlight off metal, one of the swords wielded by the leader of the group would have decapitated him and MacEwan in one swoop.

Grimaldi pushed the woman away, ordering her to run even as he took down their first assailant with a karate punch to the solar plexus, followed by a sweeping motion to the leg. The man was upended and landed hard on his back. The sound of air forced from his lungs was audible even above the clamoring and surprised crowd.

Grimaldi turned to see two of the attackers bolt in pursuit of MacEwan while their comrade attempted to distract the Stony Man ace pilot with fancy footwork and the manipulation of a large wooden staff. The attacker spun the staff high over his head at first, and then performed the same motion in front of him, dancing and thrusting his body in Grimaldi's direction, trying desperately to keep him at bay. The pilot demonstrated some footwork of his own by dropping low and executing a backward spin with his leg extended. The side of his foot caught his assailant at the ankle. It wasn't debilitating, but it was enough of a distraction so that the next move was. Grimaldi grabbed the man's still extended staff and rammed it backward into the guy's forehead. His skin split and blood sprayed onto the front of his robe. Grimaldi then rotated the stick and caught the guy in the groin before he could recover from the first blow. The man howled in anguish from the impact and doubled over. He finished him with an open-palmed strike to the side of the neck. The nonlethal blow rendered his opponent unconscious.

Grimaldi turned and looked in all directions, hoping for any sign of MacEwan. When he didn't see her, he jumped onto a nearby stall and, ignoring a protesting vendor, searched for any sudden movements. It took a few seconds, but he spotted MacEwan running back up the square in the direction they had come, the two men with swords close behind her.

Grimaldi dropped to the ground, drew the P-9 pistol from his coat and dashed off in hot pursuit.

12

Bolan didn't find what he expected upon safely reaching Musa al-Dawud's home. The old man was frenetically walking in circles as Bolan and Saura came through the door, and he immediately rushed to Saura and began speaking as rapidly as he could. There was dirt and dried sweat caked to his face, and although Bolan couldn't understand what was being said, he could detect the urgency and panic in al-Dawud's tone.

"What's going on?" he asked Saura.

"He says that your friends did not meet him as planned," she said, trying to translate over al-Dawud's chattering. "He did manage to procure all of the woman's equipment from your plane at the airport, and he says they were supposed to be at one of the tea shops in the square of the old city, but they never showed. He heard some people talking, and he thinks maybe there was—"

Bolan was already moving for the door.

"Where are you going?" Saura asked in a plaintive voice, patting al-Dawud's shoulder in a gesture of comfort before chasing after Bolan.

"I'm going to find them," he said.

"It's too dangerous."

Bolan patted the bulge beneath his jacket and said, "Leave that to me."

"What you're thinking about doing is crazy, Matt," Saura shouted from the porch of the house as Bolan climbed behind the wheel of the Land Rover, acting as if he could no longer hear the protests. "If you leave, I cannot protect you."

"I don't need your protection," Bolan snapped, fixing her with a hardened look through the open passenger window. "I need your keys."

She folded her arms and stared at him with a defiant expression. She tapped her foot, almost expectantly, but Bolan wasn't swayed.

"Look, I don't have time to argue about this, and neither do my friends."

"You are risking everything. I thought you came here to stop the NIF."

"I did, but I can't even *find* the NIF without MacEwan. Now either give me those keys or I hot-wire this thing."

"I'm going with you," she said.

"No," Bolan snapped, "you're not. I need you to stay here and keep an eye on things. If I don't come back, you'll need to get in touch with my people so they can send someone to finish the job. Now one last time, keys or hot-wire?"

Saura appeared to think about it a moment longer before pulling the keys from her skirt pocket and tossing them to Bolan through the window frame. He caught them one-handed, started the engine and got the vehicle in gear.

"You must think about this. You *must not go* without me, Matt. You do not even speak the language. You're going to need me."

Bolan thought about what she was saying, and he finally

had to agree that she was probably right. He didn't speak the language, and he didn't have the relationship with the locals that Saura probably did. It was no guarantee she could help him any more than he could help himself, but he didn't have time to chase his own tail, which would be the likely result if he went poking around where the locals felt his nose didn't belong. He definitely couldn't afford to alienate these people.

"All right, get in," he said.

When she was safely aboard, Bolan released the clutch and headed toward the market square.

"Musa said to start looking at the Qissa Khawani Bazaar, near the end of the old town," Saura told him. "His contacts believe there may be an underground sect of Afghani spies operating there."

"Why there?" Bolan asked.

"They can move relatively undetected in the *cantonment.* There is very little police activity, since there's very little crime in this part of Peshawar."

Neither Bolan nor Saura were certain where exactly in the bazaar to start their search, but Bolan figured someone had seen something, and would probably talk if the price were right.

The Executioner tried not to look out of place, but he stood so tall and moved through the crowded shops with such a purposeful stride, it was hardly worth the effort to remain inconspicuous. Bolan was a man of action. Without MacEwan, he and Kurtzman would have significant trouble tracking down the NIF's whiz kid, and Grimaldi was an invaluable asset when he needed quick air support.

So Bolan knew he had only one priority: find his allies. The rest of the mission depended on it. Bolan was at a real disadvantage not speaking the language, and he was glad he'd made the decision to let Saura tag along. She was proving quite useful with the shopkeepers and vendors lining the streets and baked mud-and-brick buildings down the central part of the bazaar.

One particular shopkeeper's words brought a smile to Saura's face, and the look she shot at Bolan told him the price for the information was worth it. Bolan quickly peeled some notes from his working stash. Saura led him outside into the sun that now sat high in the sky and had warmed the air considerably.

"What did he say?" Bolan asked.

Saura looked around before replying in a hoarse whisper, "He says that he saw two men go past about an hour ago, and there was a woman with them."

"Was it MacEwan?"

"He couldn't tell. She was wearing a traditional veil covering her face, but what he noticed was that her clothes were not the traditional dress. He thought this was strange."

"He didn't think to call the police?" Bolan asked.

"Most of the citizens in the *cantonment* are afraid of the city authorities. They have discovered in the past that if they mind their own affairs, the police will do the same. Peshawar jails are not exactly kept to the same standards as those in America."

Bolan nodded.

Saura led him through the throng, and Bolan had to struggle to keep up. There was the smell of sizzling kebabs and other delicacies on some of the open grills.

"We're here," Saura said, stopping so suddenly that Bolan nearly ran into her. She pointed at the small shop and said, "The shopkeeper said he's seen those men come and go from here on many occasions. He thinks they have a concealed area behind the shop where they conduct illicit business."

The Executioner looked at the seemingly simple facade of the storefront and then fixed Saura with an icy stare. "This is the end of the line for you. You wait out here."

"What if you need an interpreter?"

"I'll get my point across. I mean it, Saura. If I'm not out in five minutes, you go back to the Land Rover, drive away and forget you ever knew me or the others."

"But—"

"No," Bolan said before pushing through the rattan door covering. He ducked just in time to avoid smacking his head on a set of wooden chimes hanging from the ceiling.

A man seated behind a small, simple desk was scribbling something on a piece of paper. He looked up with surprise when Bolan crossed the small shop in three strides and stood over his desk. Although Bolan couldn't read the writing he was certain of one thing: it wasn't Urdu or English, the two official languages of the country. What he wrote looked more like Pashto, a Sanskrit-based form of Arabic. While Bolan didn't speak that many languages fluently, he had trained himself to know the different symbols used by a variety of languages, and to know their origins. Pashto was a language spoken almost exclusively in Afghanistan.

"Can I interest you? What you want?" the vendor managed to say.

"Yeah," Bolan said. He reached down and hauled the guy to his feet. He put his Beretta to the man's forehead. "I'm looking for an American woman, and you've got one chance—" Bolan drew the hammer on the Beretta "—to tell me where she's at."

The man began to shake. He gestured toward a wall to the right.

Bolan looked in that direction before saying, "I see a wall. So what?"

"The woman you look for behind there, behind there."

The Executioner shoved the man back in the chair and walked to the wall. He inspected it carefully and noticed a wooden stick protruding from the wall with a pot hanging on it. Bolan yanked on the stick and it moved. There was a mechanical groan, and the wall started to move. Tracking with the Beretta, Bolan risked a glance at the man to make sure he wouldn't take a club or knife while his back was turned, then moved into the darkened interior.

He looked to his right and the red, tear-filled eyes of Tyra MacEwan stared at him over duct tape securing a gag in her mouth. Bolan stepped forward and ripped away the tape, and then moments later he used a pocketknife to cut away the ropes binding her to a crudely fashioned stool.

"You okay?" he asked.

"I'm fine," she said in a hoarse tone, throwing her arms around him and sobbing softly on his shoulder.

"Listen, you're okay now." Bolan pushed her away and gripped her arms. "You're all right. Now I need you to take a deep breath and get it together. I need you to be calm until we get out of here. Okay?"

She looked at the grim, determined visage of the man and showed him a weak smile.

"Good," he said. "Do you know where Jack's is?"

"I don't know. I'm sorry." She took another deep breath and continued, "We got separated. The two who brought me here were chasing me, and I think Jack was chasing *them*. They caught me, and I heard him shouting at them, getting closer, and then…"

"Then what?" Bolan pressed when she paused.

"Then…I didn't hear him anymore. I didn't hear anything. I don't know what happened. I'm sorry."

Bolan wasn't sure how to take the news, since he didn't know whether his friend was alive or dead. One thing he did know was it wasn't MacEwan's fault, although it was obvious she was shouldering the blame. He didn't have time to deal with that now. The life of Jack Grimaldi was hanging in the balance somewhere, and while the Executioner had breath, he would search to the very ends of the earth to find his old friend.

They stepped back into the shop. The man was gone, but Bolan didn't care about that. He'd found MacEwan alive, and that was the only important thing. It had been his decision to bring her along, so he was responsible for her protection.

"How did you find me?" MacEwan asked.

"I'll tell you later," Bolan replied as they stepped outside. "Right now, it's time to get out of here."

Bolan found Saura waiting right where he'd left her, and she immediately stepped forward to take MacEwan by the arm. She scrutinized the American, inquiring if she was okay, and when MacEwan responded in the affirmative, Bolan hustled both of them into the street. He wanted to get out of there before drawing any more attention. Once they were safe at al-Dawud's then he'd go looking for his friend.

Damn it, Jack, where the hell are you?

THE FIRST THING Jack Grimaldi thought when he regained consciousness was how blasted much his ribs hurt. And then he thought about how thirsty he was, and that led him to thinking about the lump he could feel throbbing on the back of his head, and then that just pissed him off even more.

It all came back to him in a rush, a blur of memory. He'd just taken out two of the quartet in the square, and he'd been chasing the other two who went after MacEwan. He remembered them grabbing her, struggling with her lithe form. He recalled with some amusement that she'd bitten them, scratched, kicked and screamed, and fought them like a tiger.

Grimaldi's head was clearing. He couldn't see anything, but he knew his hands and feet were bound tightly at four points. He wasn't lying completely flat on his back; actually, it felt like he was bound at about a forty-five-degree angle. Grimaldi remembered getting real close to MacEwan and her assailants before someone or something had whacked him over the head. He cursed himself for being so stupid. The enemy had laid a trap for him, and not only did he fall into it, he also let them take MacEwan.

The Sarge was going to kill him when he found out. Of course, that was assuming their terrorist friends didn't beat the Executioner to it. Yeah, he'd screwed up royally. He should never have agreed to leave the safety of al-Dawud's house. In fact, he should have just risked going back to the airport on his own, and left MacEwan with al-Dawud. He had plausible deniability as a licensed pilot, and it was pretty unlikely any of the custom's officers could have identified him well enough to recognize he'd participated in the airport firefight.

"If you are thinking about escape, American," a deep voice with an accent said, "you might as well dispense with the notion."

Grimaldi saw the hulking shadow of a man pass in front of his eyes. He could see the light reflecting off dark eyes that peered hatefully at him. So, didn't look like he was all that popular with this crowd.

Grimaldi laughed.

A moment later, he was sorry as the man flicked his finger and there was a sudden jerking on his limbs. Grimaldi realized instantly the nature of the mistake. He was on some sort of stretch rack, and that initial delivery was a shock to his system. Another inch, and he was sure they would have pulled both shoulders out of their sockets. Grimaldi could hear the echo of his scream.

"It's not so funny now?" the man said, and he spit in Grimaldi's face. "You killed many of my people. I will like to watch you die."

"Up yours," Grimaldi said, knowing even as the words rolled off his lips it would cost him.

It did, although he was a bit more prepared for it and this time he was able to tense his muscles and resist some. Still the pain was excruciating. Were it not for the fact that the Stony Man pilot kept in tip-top shape through a regular physical and tactical training regimen, it would have been worse. Even so, while the pilot had never spent time as a POW, he'd heard the stories of men who had, and he'd even known Mack Bolan to undergo a variety of torture techniques.

Grimaldi wasn't so sure there would be a guardian angel to pull him out of this situation. He was fairly certain that he was going to die at the hands of the NIF. It wasn't going to be this day maybe, or even tomorrow, but he knew if Bolan or another Stony Man crew didn't find him soon, it would end. And if it meant giving up his friends because he could no longer take the pain, Grimaldi would find a way to off himself.

But hey, guy, you're not there yet, he reminded himself.

The stretching eased, and Grimaldi relaxed and took a slow, deep breath to encourage blood flow to his aching limbs.

"Ah, so you are spirited," the man said with a booming laugh. He slapped Grimaldi's belly and said, "This is good! I enjoy an American who will fight me, and who will not die so easily. There is more pleasure in it for me."

"Funny," Grimaldi said. "I thought you'd be more into little boys."

The man roared with anger, but instead of getting another stretch the pilot took a punch to the gut. All of the air he'd inhaled was forced suddenly and violently from him, and his lungs burned as he struggled to restore his breathing.

If I get off this rack alive, I'm going to kill this bastard.

"You apparently enjoy this kind of treatment."

Grimaldi heard the sound of a match being struck, and a few moments later he smelled the acrid scent of a cigarette. For a long time there was silence, and then the ace pilot could feel a hot, burning sensation on his stomach.

Jack Grimaldi prepared himself for discovering a whole new level of pain.

13

Stony Man Farm, Virginia

"We've got connection again," Aaron Kurtzman announced with excitement.

Brognola and Price looked up simultaneously from a file they'd been reviewing. The Stony Man cybernetics team had been on pins and needles for nearly twenty-four hours straight, and Kurtzman had been particularly nervous after losing contact with the network address and communications signals from Tyra MacEwan's portable system.

"Are they okay?" Price asked.

"Don't know yet," Kurtzman said. "I'm waiting for enough of a signal boost from the GPS to allow us to start up communications. But if her signal's transmitting and she's into the interface network I set up for her, then that means she's alive."

"Which means Bolan and Grimaldi probably are as well," Price said, showing Brognola a knowing smile.

The big Fed nodded and let out his own sigh of relief.

"She's telling me Striker's going to call through the satellite linkup," Kurtzman said.

"Put it on the speaker, Bear," Brognola ordered, "and let's make absolutely sure we're on a secure line."

"Understood, Chief."

A few minutes later, the familiar resonance of Bolan's voice filled the War Room.

"Striker, it's good to hear your voice," Brognola began.

The Executioner replied, "Ditto, but I'm afraid we'll have to waive pleasantries for the moment. Eagle's gone missing."

Brognola felt a cold knot in his stomach at that news. He turned and looked at Kurtzman, who immediately nodded and wheeled himself back to his computer.

Brognola could hear the concern in Bolan's voice.

"What happened, exactly?" Brognola asked.

"Details are sketchy, but it sounds like he went down trying to stop some dudes who tried to snatch MacEwan."

"Were they locals?" Price asked.

"Doesn't sound like it. I'm guessing NIF terrorists dressed as locals, which means they've been following our movements. I know someone had us marked from the start. First we got hit at the airport, and now this."

"What the hell is going on here?" Brognola wondered, and even as he heard the words come out of his mouth he could hear his own bitterness. "Sorry, gang, just tired."

"Understood," Bolan replied.

"Don't worry about it, Hal," Price said, placing her hand on his arm. "I think it's safe to say we're all just a little tired right now."

"Thanks." With the moment passed, Brognola asked, "Okay, Striker, you're in the thick of things there. What do you want to do?"

"Based on the intelligence my traveling companion has come up with so far, *and* understanding NIF operations here in Pakistan, I'm guessing that the NIF and their little whiz kid are holed up somewhere along the border."

"That would make sense," Price said. "Security's been doubly intense ever since American forces ejected the Taliban regime."

"Not to mention the fact that the hunt for al Qaeda members subsequently forced their military factions into the mountains."

"Which means they're probably still there," Price said.

"Then that brings me back to the original question," Brognola said, directing his voice to the ceiling. "What do you want to do?"

"I'd like to say first priority is to find Jack," Bolan replied, "but we all know the risks and realities of this thing if I don't move forward. MacEwan's managed to pick out these phantom signals. She still hasn't found the actual entry point into Carnivore, but she does think she can pinpoint the location where the NIF's chief hacker is operating from."

Brognola nodded, understanding where his friend was going with this. "You're hoping to kill two birds with one stone."

"Yeah. I take this whiz kid alive, provided he even exists, and simultaneously I'll bring the house down on whoever's behind NIF activities here."

"I hate to even broach the subject, but I think we need to talk about contingencies," Price said. "If you find this terrorist hacker, but no Jack, how are you going to get out of the country in one piece?"

"She's got a point," Brognola said. "It's going to be tough enough just getting MacEwan and yourself out of there, let alone dragging a terrorist along with you for the ride."

Bolan replied, "Agreed, but I'll have to cross that bridge

when I come to it. These contacts you provided seem to have one ear to the ground at all times. They managed to get me weapons and a safe place to hole up until I'm ready to go. I think they'll be able to get me a lead on Jack."

"Well, if you can't find him, we may be able to get you back here via Europe. I'll start making some phone calls and seeing if the Company can help with any of this," Price said.

"Fine. I'll work the angles here at my end, and if I come up with something, I'll be in touch."

Kurtzman said, "Striker, I'm monitoring NIF communications. If they reveal Eagle's location, I'll forward the coordinates through MacEwan's portable system."

"Understood," Bolan said.

"One more thing," Price said. "I've got some information that I'm going to have Aaron send, but there's some preliminary intel I think you might want."

"Give it to me," Bolan said.

"I followed up personally on your request to check into Nicolas Lenzini's activities, and you won't believe what we found."

"Try me."

"The guy's been running around the country, buying up all of the failing dotcom companies he can find. We started using local FBI and law-enforcement personnel to run down former employees of these companies, and what we're getting back is pretty interesting."

"The first thing Lenzini does is fire every employee of these companies before the ink's dry on the contracts," Brognola offered in way of explanation.

"So naturally most of these people are happy to talk to you in hopes of doing a little damage," Bolan finished.

"Precisely."

Price continued, "There's two very interesting things about Lenzini's activities. Everyone we've talked to so far is consistent about the fact that Lenzini seems interested only in those companies that provide Internet services. Especially those that do Web page hosting, or provide international server space to support off-site employees traveling around the world for small corporations. The list is practically endless. If it was small and crumbling financially, word on the street is that Lenzini's buying it, and he's doing it for undisclosed amounts with very little fanfare to the press."

"That sounds a little outside his normal routine," Bolan said, the tone in his voice betraying his skepticism. "I'm not buying that he's trying to go legit."

"Neither are we," Brognola said.

"Does he have any backers in this little game he's running?"

"No," Price replied.

"Okay, so that rules out either laundering or corporate fraud as a motive. You said there were two interesting things, Barb. What was the second?"

"Hardware," Kurtzman said, not missing a beat. "Lenzini's always interested in how much hardware these companies have. Particularly routers, hubs, cabling, and server racks containing space in the thousands and even hundreds of thousands of gigabytes."

"What's your assessment on that, Hal?"

"We think it could be a move toward some type of black market ops," Brognola replied. "Perhaps he needs to make some fast cash, so he looks for liquid assets he can turn around quick and make cash."

"That's a good theory," Bolan said, "but something about

this whole thing still stinks. I'm going to have to give it some thought and see what I can come up with."

"We'll do the same here," Price replied.

"Okay, I'd better go."

"Watch yourself, Striker," Brognola said. "I have the feeling this is much bigger than we first thought it was."

"Yeah," Bolan said. "I was just thinking the same thing."

There was a click and the Executioner was gone.

Brognola shook his head. The New Islamic Front had a faction operating in the U.S., and Stony Man didn't have the first idea who was behind it all. Then, to make matters worse, one of the most sinister and powerful syndicate leaders in D.C.'s history was running around and gobbling up every crumbling piece of technology he could find. And it all pointed to one thing: the Internet. It just didn't make sense. If the intent of the NIF was to crack the security in Carnivore, what did they need the Internet for? No, it didn't make a damn bit of sense.

Now Jack Grimaldi had disappeared, and while Hal Brognola didn't want to admit it, the war against the NIF had just gotten personal.

Afghanistan

SADIQ RHATIB GREETED his uncle warmly. The two embraced under the watchful, penetrating gaze of Khayyat Malik. The colonel had obviously been happy to see him, and that made Rhatib feel much better. The border crossing had been a bit laborious and frightening, but Rhatib was now feeling relaxed, and comfortable in the safe and secure confines of the mountain camp.

For three years, this had been his home. Rhatib loved Afghanistan, and he hoped someday that he could walk freely through the streets of its grand villages and cities without worrying about someone threatening his life at gunpoint because he held firm to his religious and political convictions. Many of those in the West thought that Islam used a political platform to enforce their religious dogma, and perhaps that was true of some of the radicals. But Rhatib did not believe in mixing his religious convictions with his political ideals.

Killing Americans outright by bombing commercial buildings and hijacking aircraft was a waste of time. His way was a *better* way. You let the Americans develop and build their technologies, and then you used those to control them. Such practices had proved successful against the Americans time and again, and there were many who had proved it. The Japanese proved it when bombing Pearl Harbor, and Saddam proved it by setting oil fields ablaze and dumping chemicals in the air without U.S. troops being aware it was done.

Rhatib loved his uncle, but he did not wholly agree with Abdalrahman's preaching that jihad, and only jihad, against the Americans was the key to restoring Afghanistan, the Taliban, the Islamic tradition. These were the policies to which Malik and his men clung, and it disturbed Rhatib. He wanted a peaceful means to resolving the conflict. Even when he did get control of American defense systems, he would not allow his uncle or the puppet governments funding the operations to actually use these weapons against the Americans. A mere demonstration would be enough to bring them to their knees. U.S. citizens would pay anything and do anything to avoid having their precious country blown to dust.

"You're so quiet," Abdalrahman said.

Rhatib turned, startled to see his uncle standing in the

doorway of his bedroom. Rhatib had been staring through the wooden frame of the mountain retreat, watching the distant, twinkling lights of Jalalabad far below them. A sudden, biting breeze blew in his face and he decided to close the window and keep in the heat that rolled from the burning wood that crackled in the stove.

"Malik says you've been quiet since you left America," Abdalrahman added.

"It is by no intent meant as disrespect."

Abdalrahman chuckled. "Of course not. I never thought it was." He stepped into the room and closed the door behind him. He went over to the bed and sat on the edge, patting the thick blankets next to him and watching his nephew.

"I am very tired, Uncle."

"I understand," he said. "And I have every intention of letting you rest. But I have been lonely without you. I just want to talk to you. Come sit next to me. How is your work progressing?"

Rhatib took a deep breath before replying. "It is going well. I think that we should have full control of the FBI's systems within a few days, and before the end of the week, I will be able to interface with the American defense systems of both major naval elements in their Third Pacific Fleet, and their missile control defense systems that they claim they do not have off the coast of Japan."

"This is fantastic news!" Abdalrahman said, clapping his hands. "You have done so well. My brother would have been very proud of what you've accomplished for our people, Sadiq."

"I would not have been able to do this without your guidance and support," Rhatib replied with a respect he didn't really feel.

Rhatib had never really had much appreciation for their relationship. He knew he was much more intelligent than his uncle. He also knew that despite his uncle's favor, Abdalrahman was quite capable of another tact entirely, and could become hateful and violent with little or no provocation.

"Has Malik managed to extract any information from the American pilot?" Rhatib asked.

Abdalrahman shook his head and rose, walking to the window and opening the heavy wooden doors, seemingly ignorant to the fact that Rhatib had just closed them to keep out the sudden drop in temperature. There were times when his uncle could be nothing short of absentminded, and yet he was a brilliant military tactician and the bravest soldier Rhatib had ever known. There was such a dichotomy to his uncle's personality. He was a complicated man.

"I'm confident that Malik will bring the American around to our way of thinking," Abdalrahman said. He turned and looked at Rhatib, adding, "Malik is quite talented in that way. Wouldn't you agree?"

"I would."

"Blast, Rhatib! What's wrong with you, boy? You seemed happy when you left, but now you seem so empty!"

Rhatib shrank under the baleful stare, and Abdalrahman had to have realized he was yelling because he suddenly lowered his voice and some of the redness left his face. In fact, his expression became almost timid, his voice soothing, and he slowly returned to the bed and gingerly sat next to Rhatib.

"I am sorry, Nephew. It is not like me to speak to you that way, I know. It is just that I am under significant pressures. These pressures are outside of your control, and it is my failure. I must learn to control my temper. I am sorry, and please believe when I say that it is not your fault. You do believe me?"

"Of course I believe you, Uncle," he replied. "I have *always* believed you."

"That is good. So tell me about the rest of the plan. How are things proceeding with Lenzini?"

"Malik handled most of the affairs with this American. I personally do not trust him. I think he would turn on us if given half an opportunity. He is an imperialist dog and a Westerner, and you know as I do that they are not to be trusted."

"Hush, Nephew. That is not of your concern. Once we have what we need, I will make sure that Lenzini is taken care of. Just like our other contacts there. In the meantime, your focus should remain where it has been. You are our secret weapon against the Americans. Your work is of the most importance to our efforts."

"I understand," Rhatib said. This time, he had some feeling about it. Abdalrahman, despite his many faults, also had many good qualities, and it was at these times that Rhatib admired him most. "You are always good at making me feel better."

"I love you, Rhatib," Abdalrahman replied. "You are my flesh and blood, and I promised your father that I would take care of you. With his last breath, Rhatib, your father's only thoughts were for you and your mother. Ultimately, I could not protect her. All I could do was make sure that you lived a long and prosperous life, free to go anywhere in this country and do anything you wished. That is still my goal."

"You have sacrificed much for our people," Rhatib said. "I hope some day that they honor and respect you appropriately for it. I will make sure of this. When our country and our people are whole again, Uncle, I will make sure they remember the name of Umar Abdalrahman."

"Now it is your words that comfort me."

"Uncle…"

"Yes, what is it, Rhatib? Speak up and make sure you are heard. One day you will take my place as a leader of men, and you cannot incessantly mutter and mumble."

"This man that Malik has told me about," Rhatib said, biting his lower lip a moment before continuing. "This man is dangerous. I have seen him fight. You, of course, are much better but I am still concerned."

"Malik already told me about this American."

"He haunts my dreams. He won't find us, will he?"

"If he comes here, I will destroy him with my bare hands," the older man said.

"I have seen this man fight," Rhatib said, even in the full knowledge that he was pressing an issue that Abdalrahman obviously didn't want to discuss. "I watched him kill more than a dozen of Malik's guards. He is *dangerous*. I want you to find him and kill him now. I don't want him to come here."

"You are being foolish, Rhatib. This man has no idea where we are. And even if he did, he would not dare try to attack us. There are over one hundred of our finest troops here. He will not come."

But even as Abdalrahman tried to reassure him, Rhatib wasn't convinced. The American *would* come. Rhatib had seen it in his dreams. He'd seen the fiery visage and cold, blue eyes of the American warrior, and he'd watched the face melt into that of a skull—the head of Death. It did not matter what Abdalrahman thought, or Malik thought.

The American would come.

14

Mack Bolan watched the area ahead of him with concern, and the closer they got to Jamrud Fort, the less he liked this plan.

It wasn't that the Executioner didn't trust Saura and al-Dawud, but they would be dealing with the Pakistani military. They weren't a bunch of dumb, raw recruits, they were hardened veterans and soldiers. The Pakistani army was a force with which to be reckoned, and Bolan had the utmost respect for them. They were tough, experienced, and not willing to put up with a whole lot of crap from a bunch of outsiders making worse an already hostile and unstable situation. Especially when those outsiders were Americans. Bolan knew if army regulars caught him, he'd be shot immediately—and that would end his little excursion into the Afghanistan countryside *real* quick. He just hoped this crazy scheme Saura had cooked up worked.

The ride beneath the dusty, burlap canopy was hot, bumpy and uncomfortable. Even though the outside air temperature was quite cool, the noonday sun beating down on the burlap beneath which Bolan lay was brutal. Drops of sweat poured from his face, mixing with the coating of dust around him, and when mixed the two became a mud that had now managed to cake just about everything around him.

The cart, which was drawn by a pair of donkeys, rocked back and forth and to and fro like a basket on top of a camel. Al-Dawud had bought the thing for what amounted to only two hundred U.S. dollars, making their cover complete and some cart vendor an extremely wealthy and happy man. Like Afghanistan, poverty ran rampant in most of Pakistan.

"We are approaching the Bab-i-Khyber," al-Dawud called in a tense voice, just loud enough for him to hear.

That was good news. Once they were on the other side, the Executioner would be able to get out from under his hiding spot and progress onward toward Afghani country. Jamrud Fort was the farthest point anyone was allowed without permits from the Civil Secretariat. Just like the arms-producing village of Zarghun Khel, travel through the Khyber Pass nestled in the Suleiman Hills was not exactly promoted by the Pakistani government.

Nonetheless, Bolan's trip wouldn't be an easy one. It was winter, which made any public travel along parts of the road treacherous at best. Once they were beyond Jamrud Fort, they would proceed through the Khyber Pass as far as the Afghan border, or at least as far as they could get with their antiquated cart, and then Bolan would have to continue on foot until he reached the area pinpointed by MacEwan as the most likely source of the NIF signals, and which was also Grimaldi's probable location. All the evidence and rumors pointed to that area, so the Executioner was going to concentrate everything he had on it.

With a bit of luck, al-Dawud had managed to get the explosives from the Stony Man plane, so Bolan at least had the remaining WPs and the explosives satchel he'd brought to Pakistan, which included five pounds of C-4 plastique, some detonators, two hundred feet of det cord, and a remote trigger. It wasn't much but it could certainly make a dent, and the warrior could be happy for that. It was certainly enough for its intended use, which was to blow the NIF's sensitive electronics equipment straight to hell.

Yeah, it would do nicely for that job.

Bolan also had the Galil replica locked and loaded, and strapped across his back. The Beretta rode in place beneath his left armpit, and the CAWS was positioned and tacked down as a rear weapon. In the event someone tried to crawl up and into the cart itself, they would be in for a very rude awakening, buckshot style.

Bolan's mind was on the safe retrieval and return of Jack Grimaldi. Bolan could imagine what horrors the guy might be suffering—and *those* were imaginings he could have done without—but he'd sworn he would do all in his power to pull his friend out of it alive. He meant to keep that promise.

"Here we go," Saura whispered.

Through a small slit in the burlap, Bolan could see that a Pakistani army officer had his hand raised and was ordering the cart to stop. Bolan knew that Saura and al-Dawud would be speaking to the group in Urdu, the national language of the country, which both were quite fluent in. Bolan really didn't know much about the language, but he did know his benefactors would appear quite "local" to the Pakistani officials, and that was all he could hope for.

What made Bolan most nervous even as they began to talk to the soldiers was that he couldn't understand a word they were saying. If trouble started, he wouldn't know anything about it, and that meant he'd have to play the next few minutes by ear. Of course, that's what he'd done before so what else was new?

The conversation seemed to take a normal turn for a minute or two, but then there was what sounded like a change in pitch in the voice of one of the troops. Bolan couldn't see who was speaking, but he could tell something was up and it wasn't good. Bolan felt the cart rock with movements just outside the burlap tarp.

Saura and al-Dawud were being forced to disembark from their rickety old ride.

Bolan slowly reached beneath his body and palmed the Beretta, licking the sweat from his lips. It was salty and bitter against his tongue, and he could tell he'd taken his first steps toward dehydration.

The Executioner tensed as he felt the cart shake again, this time caused by troops climbing on the side and the back. Bolan waited for the moment when they would rip back the tarp and find him there. He wasn't sure he could bring himself to shoot unprepared soldiers who were just doing their jobs to the best of their abilities. No, he couldn't kill them. It wasn't right.

Bolan could see the waist of one of the soldiers who was standing in the front of the cart. The Executioner bit his lip as a rifle butt smacked into his lower back. The soldier was jabbing at the canvas, trying to get a reaction. He jabbed once…twice…a third time—he was about to get a reaction when something odd happened. Bolan's world suddenly became an explosion of red as the soldier's belly exploded and sprayed his guts against the burlap. Bolan heard the familiar sounds of bullets impacting on flesh, and then he heard the man scream with agony before his body slumped forward, all of his weight crashing on top of Bolan.

The Executioner didn't know what was happening, and at first he thought that al-Dawud had jumped the gun and started an all-out battle with the Pakistani troops. That didn't make any sense, though. If he knew anything about the older man, it was that he was experienced enough not to start trouble before it was needed. Al-Dawud would have waited for them to discover Bolan before he reacted.

No, there had to be another explanation.

Bolan yanked on the quick release knots he'd taught al-Dawud to use so he would be able to escape with ease. Muscular arms pushed upward, tossing the body of the soldier completely off the cart. Bolan came to his knees and looked around, immediately aware that the Pakistani guards were no longer focused on the cart. Instead, they were behind cover and had taken up firing positions in the direction of the city.

Two older utility pickups, British-made with UN markings, were speeding along the main road, weaving a crazy but purposeful path to avoid the hail of automatic rifle fire now directed toward them by the Pakistani troops. The drivers of the trucks kept their heads low while those in the back leaned out the sides and returned fire with a variety of automatic rifles and machine pistols. They were dressed similarly to the group Bolan had encountered in the airport, and that left no doubt in his mind as to the identities of the new arrivals.

Bolan holstered the Beretta while bringing the Galil off his back. He put the weapon in battery and went flat to his belly. Bolan aligned his sights with the driver of the closest truck, which was within a few dozen yards of the cart, and carefully verified his target before squeezing the trigger. The Galil replica was a respectable weapon as far as Bolan was concerned. It still chambered the traditional 7.62 mm NATO rounds and was so accurate in its representation that it even had the folding metal stock of the AR version.

The Executioner's mark was true. All three of his rounds struck head-on, the first punching through the windshield, which predated the safety glass installed in later models of the truck. The entire thing exploded, raining glass everywhere as the other two rounds hammered into the driver's upper lip and nose. Bolan could see the terrorist's head explode. The driverless truck began to bounce and swerve in every direction. It looked like it was going to go off the road and miss the cart entirely, but at the last minute a back wheel grazed a boulder and the truck skidded back on course.

All Bolan could do was brace himself as the truck crashed into the side of the cart. The donkeys brayed as the weight of the cart shifted. The top-heavy design caused enough of a shift that the cart couldn't maintain stability on the rickety wheels and Bolan could feel himself sliding toward the ground with absolutely no control. The sensation was strange, almost as if the cart were upending in slow motion, but Bolan knew his best chance was to simply prepare for the landing.

Bolan hit the ground feet first, Galil braced in front of him, and as the sounds of the contents spilling from the cart and crashing to the ground reached his ears, he was already rolling out of the fall. He came to his feet in time to turn and see two Pakistani soldiers being crushed beneath the cart, their fates matched by a pair of NIF terrorists unprepared for the impact who sailed over the top and landed headfirst on the stony, dry ground. Bolan could tell the force of the trauma had broken their necks on impact.

The Executioner went to one knee, raised the Galil and squeezed off two controlled bursts at the terrorists now bailing from the pickup truck. One twisted and danced under the impact of the heavy caliber NATO slugs, red dots peppering his white garb, the blood pouring from the holes and staining the entire fabric scarlet within moments.

Bolan caught a second terrorist with a full blast to the chest. Blood and frothy sputum erupted from his mouth, and he dropped to his knees, weapon forgotten as he reached for his throat. The guy gasped for air one last time before tumbling onto his side and twitching as his brain took what little bit of oxygen remained to tell him he was as good as dead.

The remaining terrorist happened to get lucky with a wounded Pakistani soldier whose arm was pinned beneath the cart. The NIF terror-monger grinned with glee as he pointed his machine pistol at the soldier and triggered a sustained blast of rounds into the soldier's body. Bolan grimaced from the senseless act, a pang of guilt washing through him as he realized he'd been too late to save the helpless soldier. Still, he could do one thing for the guy, and that was to insure the terrorist standing above him had just committed his last murder.

Bolan took the terrorist with a single short burst. The NIF killer's body stiffened, his grin turning to an expression of surprise as he realized he'd just become the next casualty of the battle. The rounds mercilessly ripped through flesh and bone, imploding organs and leaving exit holes the size of baseballs. The terrorist fell immediately to the ground.

The other pickup truck had stopped and a fresh torrent of NIF terrorists bailed. The terrorists were searching for cover, but they didn't find much. The driver realized his mistake, put the truck in reverse and exited. His comrades, now left without cover or a method of escape, began to scream at the retreating driver. The cowardly truck operator didn't stop.

Bolan took the moment to reply in his own expression of outrage. He leveled the Galil at his hip and began to sweep the muzzle in a corkscrew pattern, spraying the terrorists with a torrent of rounds while he advanced on their vulnerable positions. Two fell immediately under the onslaught, one taking several slugs to his legs, the other looking down with surprise as his guts spilled from his abdomen.

The soldier's eyes flicked in every direction, looking for any sign of Saura or al-Dawud, but he didn't see them. That left three possibilities: they had already been overcome by the terrorists, they were bullet-riddled and their bodies were concealed by the rocky earth and tall, wheatlike grass and shrubs growing up to the road, or they'd been crushed beneath the wagon. Bolan hoped he was wrong on all of those counts.

The Executioner continued firing his weapon while reaching up to his equipment belt and retrieving an M-15 grenade. He hooked the pin through the clip of an unlocked carabiner and yanked downward to extract the pin. He turned his attention to the donkeys, which were braying furiously under the weight of the twisted and mangled cart. He found the spot where they were hitched, and a few well-placed rounds freed the distressed animals. Bolan then released the grenade and went for cover as the terrorists tried to take advantage of his momentary distraction.

The grenade exploded as the terrorists' rounds whizzed overhead or sent splinters of wood flying from the cart Bolan now hid behind. The incessant chattering of automatic rifles and machine pistols was suddenly replaced by the screams of terrorists. Bolan could smell the scorched flesh and clothing carried on the open, cool breezes blowing across the brown, rocky plains that bordered the pass. The Executioner rose from cover and headed toward the flaming misery, pumping mercy shots into those still alive. Some were walking around in circles swatting at the offensive chemical burning their skin while others rolled on the ground trying to smother flames.

The Executioner caught a sudden movement in his peripheral vision. He turned his weapon in that direction, finger poised, and then held fire. Several Pakistani troops were now advancing on the terrorist group as well, and doing a neat mop-up job. They seemed unconcerned about him now, and obviously they realized he was on their side.

Bolan turned and began to sweep the area near the cart. Eventually, he found Saura. He tugged at her limp body and started to turn her over. A knife blade flashed in the sunlight, and Bolan moved his arm just in time to avoid having the tendons and arteries in his wrist slashed to hamburger.

"Whoa!" he said. "Take it easy. It's me."

Saura's eyes looked glazed, and she was panting. Bolan stayed out of reach of the knife, keeping a healthy distance and his weapon held at the ready. He knew this woman was his ally, but he wasn't sure if she believed the same of him. Slowly, something bordering on recognition came into her expression, and she lowered the knife slowly.

"I'm sorry, Matt," she said quietly. "I did not realize."

"Forget it," Bolan said, reaching out his hand and helping her to feet. He looked around and then asked her, "Where's Musa?"

She looked around and panic came across her features. "I am not certain. We were separated in the fighting."

The shooting had stopped, as the Pakistani army troops finished demolishing their enemy. The soldiers were going through the pockets of the terrorists, probably looking for identification. Bolan knew it wouldn't do them any good— they probably did, too—but if it kept them from cornering him and Saura or deterring Bolan from his mission, he was fine with it. For the moment, they seemed totally preoccupied with that task, and still had not taken the least interest in Bolan or Saura.

The pair began searching the grass and it wasn't long before Bolan found al-Dawud. Blood ran freely from his forehead where he'd fallen and struck a rock, but it was the very visible pattern of bullet holes in his chest and stomach that told the story of what had killed him.

Bolan grimaced, and he turned as Saura rushed up next to him and inhaled sharply with a slight cry of surprise. She dropped to her knees, and the Executioner could hear the soft utterances even as she checked his pulse and then tried to cover the holes with her hands. Blood seeped through her fingers, and finally her shoulders slumped. She pounded her fist on al-Dawud's chest, muttering to him in Urdu. Bolan realized that although she was a physician and had probably experienced suffering and misery of nearly every kind, that this was her first experience at personal loss—especially loss to such violence. She was used to treating the diseases brought about by poverty and starvation, not mourning the death of those lost on the battlefield.

Bolan knew that latter feeling probably better than anyone, and he waited a moment—out of respect—before hauling her to her feet.

"I'm sorry. I know he was your friend, and he was one hell of a brave soul." Bolan jerked his head in the direction of the Pakistani troops and continued, "But I have a feeling their indifference where we're concerned isn't going to last. I'd suggest we find transportation and get out of here."

Saura stared at him, her expression blank and her beautiful eyes empty, but she finally nodded her understanding.

Bolan took quick notice that the donkeys hadn't wandered too far. They'd provide the best transportation over the rough parts of Khyber Pass, and they could get fresh supplies once they were on the other side Jamrud Fort. Bolan reached down, grabbed a handful of dirt and sprinkled it over al-Dawud's forehead and chest.

"Rest in peace," he said.

Bolan turned and quickly retrieved their packs and the CAWS from the overturned cart. Saura assisted getting one of the packs onto his back, and then Bolan returned the gesture. Then he grabbed Saura's hand, spared the preoccupied Pakistani guards one last look, and headed for the pair of donkeys that seemed to be waiting to assist the two travelers in their escape.

15

Peshawar, Pakistan

Tyra MacEwan stared at her screen and tried to remain focused, but it didn't do any good. She couldn't stop thinking about the many people who were out there, risking their lives to keep her and the rest of the American public safe from terrorism. In particular, MacEwan was having a serious trouble living with the fact that the guy she knew only as Jack could be suffering unthinkable agony, and all because of her devotion to the technical sciences.

MacEwan wished she had never accepted the job with Mitch Fowler; nobody had forced her to go work with him. She'd been doing just fine on her own. She was a young, career-minded MIT graduate, top of her class, and an employee with the Information Processing and Technology Office at DARPA. She'd had friends and a life, and was well respected throughout the defense systems community. But all of that had paled in comparison when Dr. Mitchell Fowler, an FBI technologist and scientist renowned in the technology circles, had asked her to help him find the holes in Carnivore's security.

Hell, who wouldn't have jumped at a chance like that?

Not that any of that really mattered anymore. Mitch was

dead, possibly Jack, too, and Cooper and the others would most likely wind up the same way if she didn't knuckle down, find out who the hell was messing around inside Carnivore, and subsequently figure out a way to boot them out and keep them out. That was the real trick to this game.

MacEwan had finally managed to block out the fact that there were a dozen armed men scattered throughout al-Dawud's home, toting automatic rifles and ready to defend her with their lives. Not even high-ranking diplomats and dignitaries were afforded that kind of protection in Pakistan, which meant that Cooper's friends obviously considered her an important asset.

MacEwan shook herself when she realized she'd been dozing at her portable computer system, and she stood and stretched for a few minutes to get the blood circulating. After getting some hot tea and returning to her seat, she got to work.

MacEwan knew that, in some regards, they had done it to themselves—allowing someone to access Carnivore so easily. DARPA had essentially started it with their SuperNet programs. They'd wanted an easier way to coordinate their computerized defense systems, and to monitor and evaluate information exchange across the Internet. The answer had come in the form of a 200-gigabyte per second laser array transmitter that was half the width of a penny. Communicating through laser technology was the way of the future. They had already proved it was possible, and it was sure as hell more cost effective than thousands of miles of broadband cabling.

What hadn't been considered thoroughly in this new ability to transmit terabytes of information across thousands of miles in mere seconds were the security issues. Fowler had repeatedly tried to demonstrate this to the higher-ups in the

FBI, but nobody ever wanted to listen to him. Sure, MacEwan could see and listen just like everyone else. Most of Fowler's associates, while they respected his insight and knowledge, thought him somewhat of a nutcase. They were never shy about dumping his theories or writing them off as little more than the paranoid ravings of some technolunatic.

MacEwan had known a different Mitchell Fowler, and if nothing else she intended to prove that he was correct in his assumptions about Carnivore's security, and the very fact some terrorist whiz kid had gotten inside the system undetected only proved that. So really, she didn't have to prove anything because the proof was already there. Her focus had to be on *stopping* any further intrusions and exercising damage control on those that had already occurred.

An idea came to MacEwan based on a conversation she'd had with Cooper in the hotel room, and suddenly she didn't feel so good. It hadn't been possible to transmit code during a handshake between modems, but they now believed the NIF's electronics experts had found a way to do it. That had been assuming the intrusion had taken place during a modulation-demodulation data transfer. But that wasn't the case. The Carnivore system, like every other government system, was running tandem processes between standard digital to analog communications and the next generation Internet Super-Net technologies put in place by DARPA. It was entirely possible that the NIF had hacked into the Carnivore system through the NGI SuperNet, and not along standard lines!

MacEwan reran the programming script she'd pulled from Fowler's information files that identified the phantom signal. The IT expert typed furiously, running script after script and eventually filtering out the signal. She then switched bands and contrasted the wavelength properties of the signal against those of a digital-analog transmission. MacEwan sucked air through her teeth when they didn't match.

MacEwan accessed the files on her terminal at DARPA. She pulled the NGI SuperNet specifications and compared the same signals against the phantom signals. The signals used inside the SuperNet were carried along multiple lasers using a technology known as wavelength division multiplexing, whereby each signal traveled within its own unique color band with a wavelength modulation based on the data type being carried. In this case, the color band of the phantom signal was different than any other.

MacEwan immediately jumped up and down, pounding her fist on the table with a shout of victory. She had finally figured it out. She knew where the signal was being transmitted from, and she knew how to stop it. It would take some time to figure out what coding algorithm would be required to shut it down, but at least now she had it pegged.

She immediately switched the communications module to the person named Bear. She had to admit she was impressed with Bear's knowledge. Every time she asked him a question, he had an answer. At least, MacEwan was assuming Bear was a *he*. It was quite possible Bear was a woman, although Bear didn't seem like a real appropriate handle for a woman. Then again, maybe that was the idea. Either way it didn't matter, because she had accomplished her mission.

She typed into the software messenger: I figured it out! Now we just have to figure out how to pull the plug.

Bear's reply came immediately: Outstanding! Tell me how I can help.

Afghan-Pakistan border

MACK BOLAN STUDIED the border through binoculars.

It was ironic that this part of the border wasn't protected by officials of the Pakistani army, but rather by bands of guerrilla fighters on either side who weren't going to let anyone through, come hell or high water. Bolan could understand that commitment to duty, without a doubt. He didn't want to get involved in an engagement with either side. That wasn't his mission, and he damned sure didn't need the complications. The whole thing had already gotten too complicated. Most importantly, time was running out for Grimaldi—if he was still alive.

"What do you see?" Saura asked softly next to him.

As Bolan lowered the binoculars he replied, "A lot of firepower with guys ready and willing to use it. Are you sure this is the easiest way through?"

"I am very certain of this. The borders between these two countries are guarded very well. We could go around, but the terrain is treacherous this time of year. Not to mention the other dangers."

"Such as?"

"Wild animals, mines and those who feed off the flesh of others are just a few."

"Cannibals?" Bolan asked as he raised his eyebrows, cocked his head and squinted at her. "I didn't think there were any cannibals in this part of the world."

"I would imagine there are a lot of things here you know very little about." She flashed him a disarming grin.

He returned the cocksure expression and replied, "Yeah, but I'm learning every day." He looked through the binoculars again. "Going around this will eat up a lot of time. And time is one of those luxuries I don't think we have."

"What do you propose?" Saura waved in the direction of the parapets and towers lined with machine guns, and the guards who were walking along the edges of the road with mine detectors. "Surely you don't plan to engage them head-on."

"I'm a tactician, not a fool," Bolan replied.

Every car that got within one hundred feet was turned back, and it didn't look like anyone would get through until the guerrilla fighters had finished their sweep of the area. Bolan had heard stories of Afghani spies laying mines along the road, and the civilians who would get blown to bits walking along the edges while trying to keep the road clear for military vehicles. It was a harsh, miserable existence.

Bolan saw no reason to bring his war to those just fighting for their survival. No, these people had done nothing to him and he wasn't about to choose a violent means of accomplishing his mission when a peaceful one would do.

"Besides," Bolan continued, as he began to edge away from the cliff overlooking the border village, "I have another idea. We've got a way past this without firing a shot."

"And what way is that?" Saura asked.

Bolan raised his arm and pointed into the distance where a faint whistling sound could be heard, and smoke poured from the smoke stack. The train sounded another sustained blast from its whistle, and now it was Saura's turn to fix the warrior with a skeptical look of her own.

"How do you expect to get over the border on that train without being discovered? The border guards search everything."

"I don't expect to get over the border," Bolan replied. "I just need to get close."

SAURA DIDN'T HAVE any idea what Bolan was actually planning, but the Executioner liked it that way. She'd proved herself a trustworthy and competent ally, but the warrior didn't need someone second-guessing his every move.

"This isn't going to work," Saura whispered as the train approached. "Surely someone is going to catch us."

"Hardly. I don't think anybody will even notice us, and if they do they won't care," Bolan replied.

"I still don't think—"

"Look, no more arguments. Now get ready."

The train was chugging along fast enough that their timing would have to be perfect. They had their plan, and once they made their move it was all or nothing. One wrong move, one misstep or delay, and they would lose their chance for an easy way over much of the harsh geography that would bring them within about a half mile of the border.

"Are you ready?" Bolan said.

"Yes," Saura whispered, chewing on her lower lip. Bolan couldn't help but notice the fierce determination in her eyes. Once she put her mind to something, she was committed all the way, and nothing was going to dissuade her from accomplishing whatever she'd set out to do. Bolan admired that in her, because he had that same determination—not that it wasn't sometimes grim—and it kept him going.

"Now!"

Saura went over the boulder they'd hidden behind and sprinted for the train. Bolan counted to ten before starting after her. He could easily match her strides by a two-to-one factor, and that didn't account for the fact he was probably in much better physical condition. He couldn't have gone ahead of her, because she would never have caught up. Thus, she would run ahead of him, Bolan would then follow and get onto the train first, and he'd grab her as he went past.

The Executioner reached down and grabbed hold of her outstretched arm, and pulled her onto the rearmost part of the train with one, powerful sweeping motion of his arm. Saura collapsed against him, breathing heavily.

Bolan looked into her eyes and was tempted to kiss her. He could see she was feeling the same longing, but there was a twinge in his gut, something halting. He knew he couldn't let down his guard. Saura realized there was a change in him. She moved away and averted her eyes.

"I—" she began.

"Don't say anything," he said. "That was my fault. I apologize."

She looked at him now, and he thought maybe there was a tinge of anger in her expression. She didn't say anything else, although it looked like she wanted to. She simply turned and watched the endless winding of tracks pass under them. The wind was getting cold as they moved through the pass, and Bolan pulled a heavy cloak from his pack. It had belonged to al-Dawud.

And as the sky darkened, he thought of his friend.

"THIS AMERICAN WOMAN, the one from DARPA," Rhatib said to Malik.

"What of her?"

"She is quite resourceful. She's managed to crack the code and figure out how I got into their system. We must move to the contingency plan."

"We cannot do this without approval," Malik said.

"You have *my* approval!" Rhatib snapped. "We must put the contingency plan into place immediately. Do it now. Under my authority."

"But your uncle—"

"My uncle is not here, Khayyat. He has left for Baghdad, and I am in charge in his absence. Besides, with this American possibly out there and coming for us, we must move our people to their assigned areas in America. I will need their support when the time comes. Now do as I tell you."

"You know that I live only to serve and protect you," Malik said. "But as your servant, it is my duty to tell you when I believe you're making an error in judgment. This is one of those times."

"Your objection is noted and dismissed." Rhatib turned from his computer and looked at Malik. "As are you. Now go!"

Malik nodded and bowed before turning and leaving Rhatib's makeshift lab.

Rhatib turned back to his computer system with a sigh and shook his head. He was angry, both with himself and with his uncle for not taking care of this American bitch. She had countered him at every turn. He had been certain she'd be on his false trails for weeks or perhaps even a month. Now it appeared she was smarter than he'd given her credit for, and had discovered his entry point into Carnivore.

Rhatib tried rerouting his signal by scrambling it, then reassembling it at another gateway portal, but it was no use. The applications from his computer just weren't sophisticated enough. That meant reconfiguring his system to utilize a series of Lenzini's IP addresses. That was going to take some time.

In the interim, the contingency plan called for an immediate increase in perimeter defenses, and an all-out push to locate Tyra MacEwan and kill her. Rhatib was frustrated that he couldn't find her. She was using wireless communications, and while Pakistan wasn't the most technically advanced country in the region, there were certainly enough cell phones in use to make finding her a virtual impossibility.

He'd considered trying to crack the mysterious network signature that kept appearing throughout many of the computer systems, but it would either disappear before he could work on it, or his system would simply not recognize it and would report that the signature was nonrecognizable.

Rhatib refused to be beaten by this mysterious Net surfer. Anyone who could move in and out of computer networks virtually undetected was extremely advanced. That meant a lot of money and some very keen minds were behind such a system.

Rhatib had started collecting information each time the signature appeared, and he had been running seven or eight different decryption algorithms against the stored data on a stand-alone system. He hadn't been able to get more than a few letters or numbers from the network or IP signature addresses, and that was hardly enough. To have written a security protocol so advanced that a computer running multiple decryption programs could not crack that protocol for several weeks running was a feat of unsurpassed technical achievement.

Still, Rhatib was persistent. He'd graduated from one of the finest technical universities in the world—courtesy of an American exchange program—and now he was using the skills the Westerners had taught him to bring them to their knees. Several professors had begged Rhatib to stay for graduate studies, and a few had even tried to keep him in the country permanently, but Rhatib resisted. He'd learned enough to make his tactics effective, and he was as good as most any that the American government could throw at him.

It wasn't ego, really. It was just a matter of undeniable fact, and if…

A low hooting sound issued suddenly from a computer across the room. Rhatib instantly recognized the sound and jumped from his stool. A rush of excitement caused his face to flush. It was the decryption computer he'd set to working on the phantom signatures. Rhatib could barely keep from slapping the side of the monitor as he waited for it to warm up.

"Hurry up, you blasted machine," he mumbled.

Finally, the screen glowed, and Rhatib thought he was seeing things. He blinked twice, shook his head to make sure he was seeing it correctly, then typed in some information and reran the algorithm history. The machine whirred and buzzed and a moment later the display output the same results. There was no mistaking the report. It read: IP, Source: United States of America

Owner: Unknown

Once again he had failed to crack the code. They would have to begin doing a search through their contacts around the areas of Pakistan and Washington to see what they could find out. Rhatib would also start searching that name in the Carnivore databases.

Somehow and some way, he was going to find out all about this phantom. And then he was going to destroy it—wherever and whatever it was.

16

Night had come, and the bitter winds whistled through the hills, chilling the Executioner to the bone.

Every ten minutes or so, he'd have to stop long enough to wait for Saura to catch up as they scrambled across the rocky terrain. It was tough going. One misstep could mean anything from a broken ankle to a tumble over a cliff. The physician was slowing him down, but the decision to bring her along hadn't really been his to begin with. It had all kind of been part of a package deal in exchange for her help, and while Bolan preferred to work alone, he'd let his concern for Grimaldi overshadow his better judgment in this case. Then again, that was the nature of his profession—you lived large and learned from it.

The howl of the wind through the treacherous and winding pass resembled the sound of wild animals crying. Bolan felt like he was hearing the cries of a thousands souls who had died in those hills over time. He had a sense of foreboding, of a task not easily accomplished. He would be glad to get away from this place. There was something here that stank of killing and blood. It was a place of death.

Bolan reached out and pulled Saura close to him. "Are you holding out all right?" he shouted over the noise.

She looked at him. Only her dark eyes were visible beneath the heavy muffler covering the rest of her lovely face. She nodded, but Bolan could see there was no conviction behind that look. She was trying to be brave, but the fact remained that this was one hell of a tough trek through such countryside, and it didn't make any sense to go on if they died from exposure before ever getting there. The Executioner had to admit he was a bit winded, which meant Saura was probably struggling.

Bolan took her by the hand and headed for the overhang of a nearby ridge. Twice Saura nearly lost her balance, slipping on the thin layer of ice forming on the smooth rocks. It was beautiful country, but it was damnably dangerous at this time of year, and the Executioner wished he'd been able to get into the NIF terrorist camp by air rather than ground.

He found a cave in the rocks. It wasn't large, maybe fifty square feet, but it was shelter from the winds, it had a nice hollow and a natural ventilation hole through the top. Bolan was pleased at the luck of the natural shelter's construction as he dumped the pack from his back and withdrew a fire-starter kit. He shaved some magnesium into a small pile and then handed the knife and shaving block to Saura. He asked her to continue the process before grabbing a camp ax from the pack and heading out into the gale force winds once more.

The next item on the agenda was tinder. Bolan found a tree about a hundred yards from the shelter. It wasn't large but it was enough to get a fire going, and the branches were thick enough that they would probably provide enough time and heat until the stormy weather passed.

Fifteen minutes elapsed before Bolan came away with the prize. He returned to the rock shelter to find a perfect pile of magnesium shavings ready for lighting. Bolan quickly got the fire going.

"You have done this before?" Saura asked with an amused glance.

Bolan chuckled as he sat with his back to the wall. "A few times."

"I believe it would have been better to fly into this country," she said matter-of-factly, almost as if she had been reading the Executioner's mind.

"Yeah, I would have preferred that," Bolan said. "But with my friend out of the loop, it wasn't practical or expedient. And I don't trust anyone else to get me inside the NIF's campsite in one piece."

"I understand your problem," Saura said.

"What about you?" Bolan asked as he removed his hands from the thin, neoprene gloves he'd brought and rubbed them in front of the rising flames. "This doesn't really seem like your line of work. Why didn't you stay behind?"

"I feel responsible for your friend. I was the one who left him and your woman with al-Dawud. The health of them all is my responsibility."

"Keep thinking like that, you'll lose your sanity," Bolan said. "I used to think I was responsible for everyone. Once."

She cocked her head and studied him with interest. "And why do you no longer believe this?"

Bolan shrugged. "I guess I finally realized that things happen for a reason, and I can only be in control of what I do, not what anyone else does. And I'm not going to be responsible for those who can be responsible for themselves. Taking care of the helpless is a plenty big job in its own right."

"Ah, so you are a crusader," she said, slapping her thigh. It wasn't done in a mocking way.

"I'm a soldier. But if that makes it easier for you to accept what I do...okay."

"I do not judge you for what you do, Matt."

"You don't understand," Bolan said. "I don't really care if you judge me or not. I do what's necessary, and I do it because there are few else who are willing to do it."

She nodded, then asked, "Are there others like you back in America?"

The question seemed a bit offhanded to Bolan, given the circumstances, but he didn't mind answering in the affirmative, making it clear that the number was small.

"How long do you think it will take us to get to the camp?" Saura asked, changing the subject.

"We can't be far," Bolan said, reaching into his supply pack and retrieving the map Kurtzman had sent to him electronically. He broke out a measuring compass and then moved closer to Saura. She leaned in to look at the map with him. He kept his mind focused on the mission, trying to ignore the sensuous and undeniable attraction.

"We're here, on this ridge," he began, pointing to a section of the map. "Immediately below us there's a saddle and the central part flattens out. The intel my people pulled indicates something set up there. Satellite positioning doesn't show any heat signatures, so I'm guessing they're dug pretty well into the rock and they've erected some kind of shielding."

"I see," she said, nodding. "Your friends seem quite advanced."

"They're pretty sharp cookies," he said.

This produced a laugh from her. "This is one thing I learned about Americans. They have very strange and wonderful expressions of speech."

"We aim to amuse, I guess," Bolan said.

"I find it charming," she countered, and then she grabbed his jaw and planted a firm but quick kiss on his lips.

Bolan was taken aback by the gesture, but he simply stared at her—speechless—as the dark eyes sparkled at him. Saura was unlike any woman Bolan had ever met. She was serious while somehow possessing an attitude of good nature, and full of surprises.

"We'd better get some sleep," Bolan said.

"Will you stay close to me?" she whispered.

"I'm not going anywhere."

BOLAN WAS UP AT FIRST light and had packed by the time Saura stirred from her sleep. She saw that he was preparing to leave, so she climbed from under her blanket, rolled the covering and handed it to him, and prepared herself to depart.

The Executioner used a portable shovel to dig a hole and bury the soot and ashes from the fire. Once that was done and the hole re-covered, Bolan dragged some rocks across the soft, sandy soil to mask the fact any human had ever inhabited the place. He replaced the tools before hauling the pack onto his back.

It was still a bit chilly, but the winds had died somewhat, and Bolan knew the temperature would rise as rapidly as the sun.

"We should reach the camp by midday. Let's go."

They continued on the path they'd been traversing the night before. Bolan didn't need the map for anything more than a general guide and to keep him apprised of the kind of terrain to be encountered. He'd memorized the coordinates before leaving Peshawar, and the compass hooked to his load-bearing equipment kept them headed in the right direction. They'd gone for about an hour when Bolan suddenly sensed danger.

He stopped in his tracks.

Saura bumped into him. "I am sorry," she said. "I did not see you stop."

Bolan raised a cautionary hand. "Don't take another step in any direction. Just stand still. Okay?"

"What is it?"

"We're in the middle of a minefield," he replied tersely.

Saura looked around, trying to see any signs of it, but her expression said she didn't see a thing. She looked at Bolan, not sure what evidence he had to support his statement.

Bolan didn't say a word. He bent, looked around them and then pointed to an area just beyond a stone that was just a little too white to be sun-bleached. Saura crouched and looked to where he was pointing, and Bolan moved his finger ever so slightly to one side. Saura's eyes followed the gesture and she was about to give up when she saw them. Three little metal prongs sticking out the ground, barely visible, but there all the same.

"How did you know?" she asked, looking at him incredulously.

"Experience," Bolan said as he rose and helped her to her feet by gripping her elbow. "I saw the reflection of sunlight off metal. None of the geology in this area is really metallurgical in nature, which leaves only one assumption."

"But why would anyone plant mines that visible?"

"It wasn't the mines that gave it away," he said. "It was the sunlight reflecting off of shrapnel from mines that have self-detonated, and the pattern of rock. If you look at that area the right way, you can see the reflections and you can also see that there are no rocks around it. The pattern is too regular to be natural, hence, mines."

Bolan went to one knee, about to pull a stick from the ground to use as a probe, when a new source of reflection caught his eye from the cliffs above them. He looked up in time to see a tribesman raise a rifle and aim it in their direction. Bolan yanked Saura to the ground just in time to avoid a burst of autofire from the ambusher's weapon.

Bolan grabbed her hand and started running for life and limb, rounds chewing up the ground behind them. Through fate, or some miracle, they managed to get past the open area without detonating a mine. The field had to have been sparsely populated or most of the mines had degraded, detonated, or been buried too deeply by time and weather to be effective any longer.

They reached cover as another hail of gunfire raked the area around them. Bolan pushed Saura behind a large boulder and ordered her to keep her head down as he withdrew his Beretta.

"Who are they?" Saura asked.

Bolan brought the Beretta to his chest and without taking his eyes off the sniper's position he replied, "I was hoping you could tell me."

Bolan turned as he heard the sound of rocks and sand shifting on the hill behind them. An entire group of fighters was descending the face of the hill, weapons out and held at the ready. Bolan knew that any resistance against the fighters was useless. He and Saura would be cut down before he could get off a single round from the Beretta.

"What should we do?" Saura asked.

"Surrender," Bolan said, holstering the Beretta and raising his hands.

DARK SMOKE CURLED into the noontime sky, caused by juices dripping from the carcass of a wild animal onto the red-hot coals of the spit as the rising heat slowly turned its flesh from pink to a golden tan.

The fierce warriors looked at Bolan with suspicion. During their forced, three-hour march to the camp, Saura had asked about their fate, but Bolan could only tell her not to worry and, as a woman, she was better advised to simply keep quiet.

One significant factor that gave Bolan hope was the fact that he and Saura hadn't been shot on sight. The Executioner saw the possibility of an alliance with these mujahideen fighters. He knew there were still factions of these nomadic and tribal warriors who believed in a free Afghanistan.

Some of this warrior caste didn't support the Taliban or even Northern Alliance forces any more than they had the terrorism of the Soviet attempts to rule the country. Some tribes would have just as soon killed any invaders they perceived a threat—American or otherwise—rather than be bothered with taking sides. Some were stringently political, others violent and barbaric, and still others believed in religious purity.

Nonetheless, this tribe didn't seem to consider Bolan an enemy; or if they did, they obviously didn't consider him a threat. Bolan meant to use that to his advantage.

A hulking Afghani in traditional dress—an AK-74 slung across his back and a pistol dangling from a U.S. military holster encircling his waist—studied Bolan and Saura with interest. He was attired in the traditional brown robe and headdress of his people, and his dirty, battle-scarred face was worn and weathered by years in the harsh and merciless elements.

"You are spies," the man finally said in thick, heavily accented English.

"No, we're not," Bolan replied firmly. "We don't come with any hostile intention toward you."

"No?" the man said, and he let out a booming laugh. "Yet you come to my land carrying guns." He waved in the direction of the bag filled with weapons and explosives.

"Those aren't meant for you," the Executioner said. "I mean you no harm. My fight is with another group."

"Then why are you here?"

Bolan considered the question carefully. He knew that if he lied about his intentions, they would probably figure it out and summarily execute him. Simultaneously, they might have been friends with the NIF force hiding in the mountains nearby, in which case they would execute him. Either way, the result was the same, so it couldn't hurt to tell the truth.

"I'm looking for a group calling themselves the New Islamic Front."

The mujahideen leader looked at Bolan and something turned hard in his eyes. Bolan had triggered some emotion in the nomadic warrior. There was something dreadful—and obviously dangerous—in his expression, and the Executioner waited for the bullet as the man drew his pistol and aimed it in Saura's direction.

"I think that was not the right thing to say," Saura told Bolan.

And then Bolan heard the first shot.

17

Jack Grimaldi came suddenly awake, and the first thing he heard was the echo of his own screaming off the dungeonlike walls of his prison.

As his eyes adjusted to the gloom, he realized he'd been having nightmares of his ordeal. He began to shiver as sweat rolled down his feverish, pain-racked body. Grimaldi knew if help didn't arrive soon, he would die. At some point during one of the stretching exercises, he'd finally passed out. His chest felt like it was on fire. He remembered at least two or three times it was used as an ashtray by his chain-smoking torturer before he lost consciousness.

His gut ached from repeated blows from some unseen attacker. He was certain he had two or three cracked ribs, and it wouldn't have surprised him if he was bleeding internally from a ruptured organ or two.

Grimaldi was about to allow himself to drift off again when he suddenly felt some give on one of the ropes holding his arm. He tugged and it gave a bit more and he was able to bring his left arm down to where the thick, coarse rope was mere inches from his teeth. Still, he couldn't get it close enough that he might be able to chew his way out of his bonds. The Stony

Man pilot tried to wiggle his body—a painful exercise at best—up the rack, but the angle was too steep for him to keep from sliding down, and his feet were pinned to the rack so that he couldn't bend his knees.

Grimaldi began to scream as loud as he could. He yelled several times, calling for a guard and hoping there was someone close enough to hear him. He had to figure that in all reality his chances might have been slim to none on that count. It was entirely possible they had him locked in some deep bunker in the middle of godforsaken nowhere, and nobody would ever hear him. He'd just lay here until the flesh literally rotted off his bones.

The sound of a door opening brought hope to Grimaldi. He put his arms up as if the ropes were still tight and hoped it was dark enough that whoever approached didn't notice. A moment passed before a heavily armed, bearded monstrosity got in his face.

"How you doing?" Grimaldi cracked with a grin.

"Eh?" was all the guard said.

"You got a cigarette, man?" Grimaldi asked. Actually, he hadn't smoked in years—not that it wouldn't have been tempting right about that point, but he had other plans. "A cigarette, you know?"

"Eh?" The guy looked at him, confused, and then turned with a shrug and started to leave.

"Hey, dumb ass," Grimaldi said again, louder this time. Very slowly and deliberately he said, "Do…you…have…a…smoke?"

The guy stopped and returned to Grimaldi's side. The man's head bobbed up and down as he reached into the breast pocket of his uniform. The guard yanked a pack of Turkish cigarettes from his pocket and fished one out enough that Grimaldi could wrap his lips around it. He then struck a match until the pilot got it going. Grimaldi took a couple of tentative and easy puffs at first, not wanting to belch smoke on the first inhalation.

He nodded repeatedly, uttering "thank you" over and over to the guard. The terrorist appeared to understand, and he grinned an almost toothless smile before muttering something. Then he turned and left the room, and the clang of door rang with finality in Grimaldi's ears for nearly a minute after it was closed. The pilot waited another full minute, the cigarette stinging his eyes, and then he brought his hand down and began to burn away at the ropes.

The guard had inadvertently provided the Stony Man pilot with an escape mechanism, and it was going to cost the man more than just a cigarette.

THE SHOT DIDN'T HIT Bolan and, to the Executioner's complete surprise, it didn't hit Saura either. Instead, the mujahideen leader shot the rope on the pulley dangling above Bolan's and Saura's heads.

The effect was bone jarring as their arms, which had been suspended by the elbows on significant tension, were suddenly released. Bolan sucked in a deep breath and took the force, but he heard a sharp cry of pain from Saura. She wasn't prepared for such a rapid change in position. Bolan checked to insure she was okay. She nodded and whispered she was fine before the Executioner turned his attention to the rebel leader with a questioning glance.

Surprisingly, the man appeared to understand Bolan's quizzical expression. "You wonder why I free you?"

Bolan nodded.

"I know of this group that you seek," the man said. He lowered a hand to help Bolan to his feet, while nodding for two others to assist Saura. The Executioner accepted the gesture.

"This group," he replied. "They are not far from here."

He turned to one of his men who stepped forward with a canteen. He handed it to the leader who opened it and took a drink before handing it to Bolan. The Executioner wasn't entirely sure he could trust this guy yet, but at the moment he didn't have a choice. And he sure as hell stood little to no chance of finding the NIF camp or Grimaldi if he insulted their host.

Bolan drank a few swallows from the canteen. Saura was given some as well, and she consumed nearly the whole canteen.

"I am Sadim Jabbar, and we are the Sword of Faith," he said, gesturing to his people.

The Executioner handed the canteen to him and replied, "You can call me Cooper."

Saura tapped Bolan on the shoulder and said, "Matt, I don't think it is smart to tell them who you are or why you are here. They are most likely allies of the terrorists. The NIF supports the reestablishment of the Taliban."

"We are no friends of those you speak of, woman!" Jabbar said, spitting on the ground at her feet.

Bolan looked at her and said, "I think you'd better just listen."

Saura saw the dangerous hue of Jabbar's face, and noticed all of the other men and women who had gathered around and were staring at her. She nodded slowly and stepped back a couple of paces.

"Sorry," Bolan said to Jabbar. "She doesn't understand the situation."

"Do you know who we are?" Jabbar asked.

"I know of your group. You're called a myth in this country, but in certain circles in Europe and the United States, you're legends."

A grin split Jabbar's face and he turned to his lieutenants and translated Bolan's response. The men began to raise their rifles and pass the message onto others, and within a minute there was much rejoicing throughout the entire camp.

The Sword of Faith didn't believe Afghanistan should be run by anyone but Muslims faithful to the religion of Islam. The Koran preached peace, and these people were peaceful. The sniper on the hill could just have easily killed Bolan and Saura, but he'd chosen not to. Instead, he'd fired at them to get them to move out of the minefield and into an area where the others could take them easily and without resistance.

Jabbar's soldiers were solely devoted to him. In this nomadic tribe of warriors, he was considered both their spiritual leader and military commander. He was the head of the village and touted to be somewhat of a spiritual guide according to the studies of many anthropologists. To even be standing in their presence was a rather unique experience for the Executioner. Their beliefs paralleled his. They didn't want a war, and they used violence only to defend themselves.

"I need your help," Bolan said plainly.

"We will not confront this group you speak of," Jabbar said. "That is not our fight. Our fight is only with those who would attempt to take away our right to live."

"I'm not asking you to fight," Bolan said. "This is my battle and mine alone to wage. But I need your help to find this place. I don't have any idea where we are, since you've taken my maps. I need food and water, and I need my weapons back."

"I cannot risk my men," Jabbar replied.

"You don't have to help me," the Executioner said, sighing and trying to keep his patience. "I've already told you that this is my fight. But I have a mission to accomplish. If I don't complete that mission, a lot of people are going to die, including a very good friend."

Jabbar studied Bolan for a long time. The Executioner knew, just as Jabbar did, that if Bolan took out the NIF camp there was the possibility that the Sword of Faith would be blamed, and Jabbar would have another war on his hands. It wasn't in Jabbar's best interests to help Bolan. But there was something in that moment, something that passed between the two warriors, that led the Executioner to believe Jabbar understood Bolan's reasons for doing what he had to, even if he wasn't willing to participate in those acts.

"I shall lead you to where you need to go," Jabbar said.

Jabbar turned, addressed his men briefly, then he headed toward his tent, leaving Bolan to stand there while the soldiers circled around him stared dumbfounded at their retreating leader. Bolan turned to see the distressed look in Saura's eyes. He knew he could no longer focus on his mission while simultaneously protecting her. Not that she needed his protection. She'd handled herself pretty well outside of Jamrud, despite the fact she hadn't been armed. And she'd also made one hell of traveling companion for the Executioner. Still, it was time to part company.

"You are not taking me with you," she said.

"No."

"I understand," she said.

She stood on tiptoes and brushed his lips with hers. "I shall be okay here?"

Bolan nodded. "These are good people. They'll help you get back to Pakistan or India. Or wherever it is you're going."

"I am not yet sure where that is. Without Musa's help, I do not know how much more useful I will be to his people."

"I think you've been a lot of use to them," Bolan replied truthfully. "And I think you will again. I need you to do one thing for me as soon as possible."

"I will do anything you ask," she replied.

Bolan pulled a piece of scratch paper from his pocket and wrote a number on it. "I need you to call this number and tell whoever answers that I said to make arrangements to get MacEwan out of Pakistan if they don't hear from me within forty-eight hours. You have that?"

"I understand," she said, putting the paper in a hidden spot beneath her traveling robes.

With that, Bolan turned and headed to retrieve his packs. He hated to leave Saura behind, but it was too dangerous, and he knew that what he was about to walk into was not for people like Saura. She was about saving lives, not taking them. Bolan didn't even feel comfortable taking Jabbar with him, but he didn't have much choice in that.

This was the last leg of the trip before he dealt a crushing blow to the NIF. He damn well hoped that when it was over, and there were nothing but the ashes of the terrorists blowing away in the wind, that Jack Grimaldi would be one of those found among the living.

BOLAN WATCHED THE CAMP through the binoculars with Jabbar guiding him through the various areas.

"That is their munitions dump," Jabbar said.

"What about those posts?" Bolan asked.

"Those are walls they built on the edge of the cave entrance, and the posts are windows, " Jabbar said.

Bolan nodded, understanding Jabbar's confusing reference. "The posts are window frames. I get it. That's where I'm going to set the explosives."

"Why would you not destroy the ammunition?"

"I'll leave that stuff for you, Jabbar," Bolan said, turning and fixing his newfound ally with a grin. "I'm sure your people could use it. I don't have that much demo, and the most important thing here is to eliminate the opposition. I see no better way to do that than burying them alive."

"What is your plan?"

Bolan looked back at the mountainside camp and replied, "I'll get in, find the NIF's hacker and my friend, and then blow the place on my way out."

"You will meet much resistance. I will help you."

"No," Bolan said, shaking his head. "I go it alone from here. I won't ask you to risk your own life. You have a family and tribe to which you are responsible."

"You cannot do this alone," Jabbar said.

"You'd be surprised. Now please go back to your camp."

Bolan shook hands with Jabbar. The man seemed to disappear into the rocky terrain behind them.

The Executioner waited a minute or two to make sure he'd really left, and then he began the job of scrambling down the rocky, sandy areas on an approach vector with the camp. He'd have to come in on its flank if he were to remain undetected. He figured he was far enough out that the brush and rock would camouflage him, but as he got closer there were sentries who might spot him. He'd already marked two at the area Jabbar had described as an open staging point for choppers or vehicles.

Bolan pulled the compass and checked his position. Given distance and time, he figured he could reach the campsite within an hour, even having to divert off to one side. There were two major things to consider: patrols and mines. Either of those was a distinct possibility, given the amount of fighting that was taking place throughout the country.

On their hike to the overlook, Jabbar had told Bolan of the continuous warfare between his people and small patrols the NIF regularly sent. Jabbar always left one patroller alive to send back to the NIF's leader—a man Jabbar knew as Abdalrahman—with a message that the fighting would continue as long as the terrorists occupied the area. The Executioner knew Abdalrahman probably considered Jabbar's warriors more as troublesome, and primitive rebels than any real threat. That was pure arrogance and showed a lack of understanding of Jabbar's kind. Just like their ancestors, these mujahideen were no different. They didn't give up for anything, and they weren't intimidated by either technological or military superiority. They were fighting for ideals that most soldiers considered much more important than their own lives: freedom, duty and honor.

And they were dying for them, too.

The Executioner felt it was time to start dishing out some of what the terrorists had taken. He reached the edge of the camp within half an hour and waited nearly ten minutes before moving from cover. He low-crawled to within a few yards of the bunkerlike walls of the camp and waited expectantly. None of the sentries showed to challenge him, and there were no shouts or sounds of alarms.

Bolan would have preferred to wait until sundown, or even dawn, to plan his penetration of the camp, but he was out of time. Perhaps in some ways, his enemies were still very primitive. It was a lucky break for the Executioner, and he damn well knew it. The very fact that the NIF had chosen to rely more on ingenuity in designing and building their mountainside camp, and less on electronic security measures, made their place more vulnerable to soft probe and penetration. The terrorists had obviously become comfortable with the idea they were in the middle of nowhere, virtually undetectable by air or ground, and that was going to prove to be the reason for their downfall.

Bolan crawled the last few yards until he reached the point where he planned to set the first charge. He unwound some detonation cord from his satchel, primed a block of C-4 and wrapped the cord around the plastique. He then pressed it against the frame and set the receiver to detonate from the remote signal he would trigger on his way out.

Bolan moved to the next post and repeated this, following the perimeter until he'd exhausted his demolitions. He quickly checked the Galil replica and headed for the entrance to the camp.

It was time to find his friend.

18

Grimaldi had every intention of living, and he planned to do it by killing.

The Stony Man pilot understood that was the nature of war. They were fighting a war, and he was part of it, and now and again it meant he was called upon to do something he didn't like. Still, he was proficient with both his hands and weapons, and in boot camp and flight school he'd been instructed that a prisoner of war had only two objectives: stay alive and make every effort to escape if the opportunity arose.

I let myself get caught, Grimaldi thought.

Now he was going to get uncaught.

The cigarette lasted long enough for him to burn through both the ropes binding his hands, and now he had to find some way to free his feet. Grimaldi called once more for the guard, and it took some time before he appeared. This was a different guy, much smaller and obviously not as well fed. Grimaldi nodded at him, asking if he had a smoke while keeping his hands above him. The soldier shook his head, turned and started to walk away.

Grimaldi got the remnant of one of the ropes around the neck of the guard and jerked him backward. The pilot twisted the rope, tightening it by twisting one side over the other by repetitive motion with his hands. The move was immediately effective, cutting all air and rendering the guard unable to cry out or even speak. Well-tuned muscles tensed as the pilot yanked upward, pulling tighter and tighter. Within a couple of minutes, the body slumped entirely and collapsed to the ground.

Grimaldi reached down and searched the body until he found a curved knife with a pearl-white handle that appeared to be constructed from bone. He slashed the ropes at his feet, then stripped the guard of his bandolier and the AK-47 he'd been wearing across his back. He jacked the charging handle to the rear, insured a round was available and let it slam home.

Locked and loaded, Grimaldi zipped up his tattered flight suit and headed for the open door. He poked his head through the doorway and looked in both directions. The narrow hall was empty. The Stony Man pilot kept his back to the wall and started moving.

Grimaldi spotted a terrorist standing on the other side of the door leading from the hall. The guy tried to bring up his weapon in time, but Grimaldi had him first. The AK-47 autofire resounded like thunder inside the narrow space, causing the pilot's ears to ring, but he definitely found his mark. The short round burst hit the terrorist in the stomach and splattered his bowels against the wall behind him. The man fell to the ground with a scream, unable to control the twitching of his body as he tried to save himself by holding things together. It wasn't much help. Grimaldi put a mercy round in his head as he moved past.

Grimaldi moved beyond the hall guard and through another door. The cavelike walls were gone, replaced by an open, bright, wide hallway. Sunlight streamed through the open windows, and the ace pilot could taste the first of fresh air in what had probably been two or three days. Through the windows, Grimaldi could see ridges and cliffs of a mountain proximal to his position. He realized he was probably in some type of mountain camp that was camouflaged on its exterior.

Shouts had reached the pilot's ears, and he realized the enemy was approaching. There was the sound of boots slapping pavement. The windows were too narrow for him to fit through, and Grimaldi was positive that going back the way he came would only lead to a dead end. That meant only one thing: he'd have to stand his ground and hope the terrorists ran out of ammo before he'd expended his own. He estimated twenty-six rounds in the partially spent box, and another full magazine he'd lifted off the guard.

Grimaldi knelt behind a support post for cover and waited for the opposition to arrive.

MALIK ENTERED RHATIB'S quarters and immediately shook the young man from his bed.

"What is it?" Rhatib asked.

"My men report to me that all is in place. The woman is hiding in Peshawar, and she will be dead soon."

"And the work I asked them to start in America. Is it underway?"

"Yes."

Rhatib climbed from his bed, immediately putting on his socks and boots. The air was now warm, almost sultry, and Rhatib could see sunlight streaming through the windows.

"Is it afternoon?" he asked Malik.

"Probably," the NIF terrorist nodded. "Or very close to it.

I know that the cooks are planning to serve the midday meal very shortly."

"Then I probably have some information waiting for me." Rhatib quickly donned his traditional garb and cloak and headed down the hall of the camp's main building. Like the others, it wasn't as much a building as a series of camouflaged shelters built into the mountainside. There were hundreds of miles of caves all through the mountainous terrain of Afghanistan, and they made perfect bases of operation because they were virtually undetectable from the air or ground. Even the satellite technology in which the Americans took such stock was not capable of pinpointing the exact location of the many camps scattered throughout the country.

Rhatib implicitly trusted technology, but he also believed the user had to understand what he was using and figure out the best way to put it to use. Any who thought technology was perfect, that it couldn't make mistakes and that there was no reason something shouldn't work, were the most foolish of all. It seemed to Rhatib that many American scientists believed that.

"Ah yes!" Rhatib exclaimed, clapping his hands together as soon as he entered the room.

He moved immediately to the computer he'd been scanning and saw information had automatically printed to his system. He went to the printout and ripped it from the device. He studied it, and then looked at Malik with a smile.

"If my calculations are correct, I think I have finally discovered who sent this American."

There was a sudden sound of shouting coming from the hallway, followed by gunshots.

Rhatib backed toward the wall and Malik immediately reacted, drawing his pistol and heading toward the door.

"Lock this behind you," he said. "Do not let anyone in but me! Do you understand?"

Rhatib just nodded, and he couldn't help but jump at the sound of Malik slamming the door. He stood there a moment or two, a bit taken aback by the sound of gunshots, but then he pulled it together and went over to the door. He locked and bolted it with the upper and lower steel-reinforced bars that his uncle had installed. He had instructions to destroy his equipment if the compound was ever breached, but he couldn't bring himself to go to that extreme yet.

GRIMALDI OPENED UP with the AK-47 as soon as the first two NIF terrorists spilled through the door. He kept low to the ground, using the post as cover. As long as there were no surprises behind him, and he doubted it since there seemed to be only one way in or out of the holding area, he felt he might stand half a chance in hell of escaping.

The first burst caught one of the terrorists in the chest, punching holes through his lungs and heart. He screamed and dropped his weapon, his arms flinging out as he was pushed back against the door and fell to the earthen floor. The other terrorist was distracted long enough to meet the same fate as his comrade, the burst from Grimaldi taking him in the side. The impact spun the terrorist gunner into the exterior wall before dumping him on the ground in a heap.

Suddenly, all hell broke loose. The doorway could barely contain the terrorists that suddenly flooded the hallway, and they all triggered their weapons simultaneously. There was a cacophony of autofire, and a series of angry rounds chewed up the wooden post and spit chunks of earth into Grimaldi's eyes. The pilot rolled out of their sights and—while trying to keep from panicking—tried to brush some of the dirt and debris from his eyes.

Okay, so maybe he didn't stand as good a chance as he'd thought.

There were obviously too many to try to take all at once, especially without a grenade. Grimaldi jumped to his feet and retreated down the hallway, closing the door behind him. He propped the dead guard against it. That wouldn't hold them long, but he figured it might buy him enough time to come up with a plan.

Nothing came to him.

Grimaldi knew it was hopeless. He was at a point of put up or shut up—or in this case, die—and it seemed there was no great scheme he could conjure in that short amount of time that would pull him out of it. He watched the door slowly start to collapse under incessant blows. Grimaldi dropped to one knee, pressed the stock of the AK-47 muzzle to his shoulder and aimed it at the door.

The ace pilot didn't wait for the door to cave. He immediately triggered his weapon, and the heavy-caliber 7.62 mm rounds bored through the wood. Grimaldi couldn't hear any reaction above the hammering sound of the rifle. His senses were fully engaged by the smell of expended gunpowder and the sound of brass as it was extracted from the bolt. The weapon shook in his hands.

The AK-47 ran dry.

Grimaldi dropped the magazine, and as he reloaded his one spare he realized he didn't hear anything. There were no sounds of shouting or even of the terrorists screaming in agony. He didn't hear anyone beating against the door, and he didn't see the door moving. The pilot was dumbfounded.

He knew that his first salvo had probably taken out a couple, but he'd counted at least eight NIF gunners pouring through the last door before they'd unloaded on him. He couldn't possibly have gotten them all.

Could he?

Grimaldi went prone and prepared to open up as the door came off its hinges and slammed to the ground. He eased off the trigger when he saw the source of that swift and sudden entrance. The Stony Man pilot blinked twice, unsure if he could believe his eyes after such an ordeal at the hands of his torturers. But there was no mistaking the cold blue stare, grim visage and blacksuit of the consummate warrior.

"Well, it's about time," Grimaldi drawled.

19

Bolan and Grimaldi were headed for the exit when the Executioner stopped the pilot short.

"I have to find this NIF whiz kid," Bolan said.

"You putting me on?" Grimaldi said.

"That was always my mission here, Jack. Remember?"

"Yeah, I remember. Just you remember we need to get out of here quick like. And we need to do it *before* we bring this whole stinking camp down on our heads."

"I've already got a plan to deal with that," Bolan said. He drew their position in the dirt with his knife, then the approximate position of the landing pad. "I've mapped that landing pad a good hundred yards from here, give or take some change," Bolan said. "I've seen some sentries in that area, which tells me there's a chopper there."

Grimaldi nodded. "Agreed. Otherwise, why else put men there to guard the damn thing?"

"Exactly. I need you to get there and find it. I've cleared all of the resistance between here and the entrance to the camp, so you shouldn't have any nasty surprises. You feel up to it?"

"Yeah, no sweatski," Grimaldi said.

"Good. I'll be right behind you for pickup, plus one."

"You can count on me, " Grimaldi said. "If there's a bird out there, I'll find it."

The Executioner couldn't help but admire the pilot's guts as he threw Bolan a thumbs-up and headed off in search of the chopper they hoped was there.

The Executioner waited until Grimaldi was out of sight before turning and heading deeper into the encampment. He considered the situation, and the fact that he really had no idea who he was even looking for. Lenzini's button man back in the States had said it was a kid, but Bolan didn't know if that meant twelve or twenty.

One thing he was certain of, when he found this whiz kid, he would know it.

Bolan's thoughts suddenly shifted to more pressing matters as a few terrorists rounded the corner, weapons held at the ready. Bolan dropped and let fly with two short bursts from the Galil replica. The weapon chattered with its unusual and yet familiar sound as it spit rounds in a tight pattern. The Executioner's first burst caught two terrorists in the chests—some of the rounds going right through the first and hitting the second—while the second burst shattered a third terrorist's skull.

Bolan fired another salvo while advancing to a closer position. This one caught one of the terrorists in both the neck and chest. He danced under the onslaught, finally reaching a point where his back was against the wall, and then he slid to the ground and came to rest.

The Executioner narrowly escaped death as he dived for the ground and shoulder rolled at hearing the sound of new arrivals behind him. A hail of 9 mm Parabellum rounds whizzed over his head, and one of them nicked his thigh. Bolan rolled to his knees, turned and immediately went prone as two NIF terrorists unloaded a new series of sustained bursts from their Ingram Model 10s. The Ingram was difficult to control under sustained bursts. These users were obviously not experienced with them, because Bolan could see that they were shooting well above his head.

The Executioner leaned his cheek to the stock of the Galil as he switched the selector to single shots. He squeezed the trigger. His first round caught one of the NIF shooters in the jaw, collapsing his lower face and turning his cheeks and tongue to jelly. The impact snapped the terrorist's head and dumped him onto the ground in a heap. Bolan took the second one with two rounds to the chest. The guy stood erect for a moment, the Ingram hosing rounds into the nearby wall and ceiling, before he dropped the weapon and collapsed.

Bolan rose and checked his thigh. He was able to stand; his inspection revealed a flesh wound. He shook the pain from his mind, turned and continued in search of his quarry. There hadn't been much opposition, and Bolan was a bit concerned about that. Stony Man had estimated perhaps a hundred troops or better at the encampment, which would have comprised the majority of the NIF force. Jabbar had confirmed those numbers. Yet, he hadn't come anywhere close to meeting that type of resistance.

Yeah, something wasn't right.

Bolan came to a door and after trying the handle and finding it locked, he put his foot to it. The thing came off its hinges, the cheap wood splintered and the door went flying halfway across the room. Bolan stepped into the interior and he could hardly believe what he saw. There were computers stacked everywhere.

One row of eight was arranged on a cart and stacked in

pairs. Green lights winked on and off from every one of them. There were no terminal screens attached to them, and Bolan immediately guessed they were probably backup systems or servers. Another two systems took up an opposing wall, and looked like individual workstations. There was a desk in one corner with an eleventh computer system on it, and a stand-alone on a bench that looked like it was partially disassembled.

The room was otherwise empty. Bolan looked at his surroundings carefully and decided it was too quiet. Something told him that despite the fact there didn't appear to be any other way in or out of the room, it shouldn't be empty. The Executioner cocked his head and attuned every sense to his environment. Then he heard it: the faint sound of erratic breathing. It was coming from a corner, under a table, and the Executioner walked slowly past the area as if he were interested in something else. Bolan kept his back to the area, but he had his weapon held at the ready.

Predictably, the figure burst from its hiding place and tried to escape. The Executioner managed to reach out and haul the person up short by the back of the robe. He continued the motion and whipped the figure around, slamming it face first against the wall. The man didn't fall but instead let out a scream of terror. Bolan turned the figure and saw a young man, maybe eighteen, wearing a look of terror combined with sheer panic.

Bolan pressed the barrel of the Galil against the young man's forehead. "What's your name?"

"I will tell you nothing!" the kid said, spitting at Bolan.

"Let's go, genius," Bolan said to him, waving his weapon in the direction of the door and grabbing the kid by the arm and steering him toward it.

Bolan stopped when he saw the doorway filled with a hulking form of a man. He recognized the leader of the terrorist band from the airport. He stood there, an AKSU held at the ready.

This kid was obviously vital to the NIF's operation, and Bolan knew the behemoth in the doorway didn't plan on letting him leave with the kid as his prisoner.

"Let him go, American" the man said. "Your fight is with me."

"Malik," the kid said, "I order you to step aside and let us pass. There will be another time—"

"The time is now!" Malik said, charging them with a scream and aiming his weapon toward Bolan's head.

The Executioner pushed aside the frail, wispy frame of the young man before ducking under a hail of SMG fire. Bolan stepped forward and jammed the butt of the Galil into Malik's midsection. Air whooshed from the man's lungs but he danced to the side and appeared to quickly recover from the blow. He aimed his weapon at Bolan's head, but the Executioner managed to smash the stock against his wrist and drive the weapon from his hand.

Malik roared with anger and jumped at Bolan, producing a long, curved knife from the folds of his robe. The Executioner's weapon was useless in such close quarters, and he dropped it in time to trip Malik. The NIF terrorist had his arm over his head, ready to smash it into Bolan's skull, but he was now off balance. Bolan stepped forward, crossed his forearms and grabbed Malik's wrist before the guy could complete the move. Then the warrior simply yanked back and pulled down, which slammed Malik to the ground.

Bolan stomped his boot toward Malik's throat, but the terrorist managed to roll away just in time. He reached out and tried to grab his dropped knife, but Bolan beat him to the punch. The Executioner drove the sole of his foot onto Malik's arm. The terrorist screamed, but as Bolan reached for the knife, his adversary seized the advantage and managed to push the Executioner off balance. Bolan's fingertips brushed the knife handle as he was pushed away, but he wasn't close enough to actually take possession, and the fall knocked the wind out of him.

Malik scooted forward on his belly and managed to get to the knife. He climbed to his feet with surprising speed for his size and charged Bolan. His overconfidence proved to be his undoing. Bolan rolled onto his back and launched a snap kick that connected with Malik's groin. The man stopped suddenly, knife still held in two hands over his head, and let out a howl of agony as his testicles were crushed under Bolan's heel.

The Executioner spun onto his side and used a double leg sweep to knock Malik off his feet and dump him onto the ground. The knife bounced from his grasp and skittered across the room. Bolan rose to one knee and drove a hammer fist into Malik's solar plexus. He coughed once, the air leaving his lungs even as he tried to howl in the pain, but nothing above a squeal really came forth. Bolan drew his Beretta and finished the job with a 9 mm hollowpoint to Malik's temple.

Bolan was winded and barely prepared for what came next. The knife was flashing before his eyes as the young man was slashing at him. The soldier waited until the last possible moment and then as the knife blade whistled past, he helped it along by grabbing the kid's wrist and driving his forearm into the back of his opponent's elbow. There was a snap and the kid screamed as he dropped the knife.

The Executioner rose, forcing himself to steady his breathing as he grabbed his prisoner by the collar, retrieved the Galil and headed for the exit.

It was time to move.

GRIMALDI WAS CERTAIN that he'd exhausted his search for the chopper when he suddenly saw it camouflaged behind some netting. It was only a moment, barely the passing of a single breath, when what must have been a single ray of sunlight reflected off a blade. The rest of the thing was painted in a matte black, and Grimaldi didn't have the faintest clue how he would have ever spotted it otherwise had it not been for just plain good fortune. Getting to it would be no problem.

Grimaldi came out from his cover and took the first of four terrorist guards with the AK-47 by firing a short burst to the guard's midsection. The terrorist's scream died in the mouthful of blood that he regurgitated. The other guards began to return fire with Grimaldi, reacting admirably to the hostile ambush. The pilot rolled under a hail of slugs that buzzed past him like an angry swarm of hornets.

Grimaldi quickly found cover behind a boulder and sighted on one of terrorists. He took a deep breath and let out half, then squeezed the trigger with firm but equal pressure. It only proved to him that he'd been trained by the best when his single round crashed through a terrorist's skull and flipped him off his feet.

Grimaldi changed positions, running laterally to his opponents and firing bursts more to keep their heads down than to do any real damage. He needed to keep them pinned down until he could get into a better position to take out the remaining pair. Unfortunately, the terrorists realized that their numbers had been reduced by half within half a minute, and decided to seek cover. If they managed to settle into a reasonable area of natural terrain, they could easily keep the pilot pinned down for a while.

Grimaldi decided to charge them. He felt like a raving, suicidal maniac as he left the dense brush and boulders that had protected him and rushed into the open where he was a target. He'd never tried such an insane tactic before, and the fact he'd even made such a decision took him by surprise. It seemed to have the same effect on his enemies.

Up to that point, they had been running for cover but when they heard the screaming they turned and froze, watching as the madman advanced on them. Grimaldi couldn't believe the reaction even as he sprayed the area with AK-47 fire. One got caught in the thigh and hip, the impact spinning him away from Grimaldi. Two more slugs caught him in the lower spine and finished the job.

The remaining terrorist never even got a chance to retreat. He received a full blast to the chest. Grimaldi kept the trigger depressed as he watched flesh and bone erupt in a gory spray, the muzzle of his weapon rising and also turning the terrorist's skull to mush. He made sure his target went down and stayed that way. The guy collapsed as the blood from his chest and mutilated head began to pour freely and change colors as it mixed with the earth and rock.

Grimaldi dropped to one knee and waited nearly a full minute, steeling himself for any further resistance. It never came. The pilot finally slung his weapon, rushed to the camouflage netting and struggled to get the stuff torn free.

After he'd freed the chopper, Grimaldi realized it wouldn't do much good. The chopper was an old Cayuse OH-6. It was small, without a real long range, but it could hold up to four and that would be good enough. The problem was, even on wheels, he couldn't clear the chopper from the netting enough to get it into position on his own. He needed someone to assist, and he had no idea under what conditions the Executioner would be coming, whether alone or with eight million screaming terrorists in hot pursuit. The latter scenario was the one Grimaldi envisioned as the most likely.

As if in answer, Bolan suddenly appeared at the rise to the landing pad with a young-looking man accompanying him. Grimaldi began to shout and wave his arms, but he was cut short by the sound of automatic fire. The pilot turned to see several terrorists approaching from another point. Grimaldi retrieved his AK-47 and began to put out covering fire.

Bolan took the risk of crossing the flat clearing of the makeshift pad with his prisoner in tow. He reached the chopper and shoved the young man in Grimaldi's direction. The pilot caught the kid without missing a beat and shoved him toward the cover of the chopper.

"What's the delay, ace?" Bolan asked.

"It's too heavy. I've got to get into a clear position or we'll suck all of this netting right into the rotors!" Grimaldi shouted, ducking to the side in order to avoid a fresh hail of autofire.

Bolan nodded, then turned his attention to the problem at hand. There were at least a couple dozen terrorists coming down from an overhanging hill, and because they had the advantage of both cover and higher elevation, the Executioner figured the odds of survival weren't great. But they still had enough distance that they could risk putting the chopper in position.

"Come on," he told Grimaldi. "I'll give you hand."

Bolan rushed to the Cayuse and opened the door. He

grabbed the kid, punched him behind the ear to render him unconscious and tossed him inside the rear compartment. He and Grimaldi then pushed on the Cayuse with all of their might. The chopper wheels groaned at first but as the pair picked up speed, they cleared the netting and put the chopper into a position to make Grimaldi comfortable for a clean take-off. The Executioner didn't have to tell him to start the engines. The pilot immediately jumped inside and began to flip switches.

By that time, the terrorists were in effective firing range. Bolan moved away from the chopper, trying to draw their fire. He figured they hadn't gone to such trouble to set a trap when they could have just as easily taken them at the camp. No, this was probably a group returning from patrol—maybe even a couple of groups given their numbers.

The muzzle of Bolan's weapon was turning red hot as he traded out magazine after magazine in the Galil. He was down to his last within a couple of minutes and he'd only dropped perhaps a third of the force coming at him. He had succeeded in keeping the fire off the chopper, and he could only be thankful for that much. He wished he'd had radio contact with Grimaldi. He would have instructed the pilot to boogie and arranged a rendezvous somewhere else once he'd shed the heat.

The sound of a fresh torrent of gunfire suddenly commanded the Executioner's attention. It was coupled with the sounds of a familiar cry. Bolan looked higher into the hills and spotted Jabbar rushing down the hill behind the terrorists on their exposed flanks. Fifty or so of his men accompanied him. They came from the bushes and rocks, and they laid down a heavy fusillade. Bolan could hear the shouts of pain and surprise as the Sword of Faith rebels poured the vengeance and wrath of the thousands who had gone before them down on the NIF band.

Bolan waved and Jabbar stamped his chest with his rifle in a returned greeting. The Executioner rushed for the chopper. He hopped into the copilot's chair and flashed a grin at his friend. He was damned glad he'd pulled Grimaldi out alive.

"Sure is good to have you behind the stick," Bolan said.

The pilot grinned.

When they were high enough to see the results, Bolan removed the remote detonator from his blacksuit, keyed in the signal to arm and flipped the switch. The walls of the NIF camp exploded and, under the practical and experienced skills of the Executioner, blew in such a way that the cave rock literally collapsed around the area. There would be nothing left to suggest anything had ever been there but the remnants of a rockslide.

As they started to move away, Grimaldi inclined his head toward the rebels who were still advancing on the NIF terrorists. "Friends of yours?" he asked.

"More than you know, ace," Mack Bolan replied. "More than you know."

Epilogue

Peshawar, Pakistan

It came out of nowhere.

The sounds of automatic rifle fire jarred Tyra MacEwan from the first sound sleep she'd had in a week or more, and she rolled off the bed in time to avoid being shot full of holes. Her bodyguards were either dead or dying. They had been garroted, shot, or stabbed and there was little to no protection still standing.

Those who had escaped the initial onslaught appeared to be fighting for their own lives. It didn't seem to do much good as the cloaked invaders entered the house and attacked with the ferocity of wild animals. The last of MacEwan's bodyguards fell near her bed, which she had taken refuge beneath. His lifeless eyes seemed to stare at her as blood began to seep from his mouth.

The sight horrified MacEwan, but she resisted the urge to cry out. It probably wasn't going to do her a lot of good, hiding out as she was. The NIF gunners weren't so stupid that they wouldn't look in every nook and cranny to find her. She was as good as dead. She could expect torture before death; she was sure of this. And with Jack and Cooper missing in action, it was highly unlikely that they'd get back in time to find her. This was it. After all she'd accomplished, she'd finally reached the end of the line. She wouldn't go out without taking at least one of the bastards with her.

The bed was suddenly upended, and MacEwan's eyes stared into the face of a dark-skinned man with a beard. His eyes were bloodshot, it was obvious even in the poor light, and he stared at her hatefully behind the mask across his face. He started to reach for her, and she kicked at him. He deflected her legs easily enough and started to reach for her again.

His body suddenly stiffened, and his eyes went wide as he toppled onto her. MacEwan could feel something hot and sticky on her stomach, and when she reached down to feel the area, she withdrew a hand covered in blood. She started to scream, but the loud booming of a shotgun drowned out the sound.

The figure that suddenly flew through an open window looked like a floating, black specter of Death. In fact, it was Cooper and he was kicking ass and taking names.

MacEwan watched in amazement as Cooper first took out the gunmen, then he dropped from a rope and rolled into a crouching position a few feet from where she lay. He looked at her intently.

"You all right?" he asked.

"Yeah, I think so. There's blood on me."

"Is it yours?"

"Don't think so."

"That's good," he said, and ordered her to put her head down as he leveled the odd-looking shotgun and fired a 3-round blast in the direction of two terrorists.

Cooper yanked on her arm and hauled her toward the steps.

"Come on," he said. "We're getting out of here."

He got her to the rooftop and she was shocked to see a

small chopper touching down. The wash of rotors tossed her hair in wild directions, and her ears rang with the throbbing hum of the engine. Cooper helped her into the copilot's seat and climbed in the back.

MacEwan couldn't resist throwing her arms around Jack, and he winced before tossing her a cocksure grin.

"You're alive!" she said.

"Looks like I got Sarge here just in time to keep you in the same condition."

She was puzzled at first, but then realized that the pilot was talking about Cooper. She'd heard him call the guy "Sarge" several times before, but she hadn't understood the reference. They were probably former wartime colleagues, perhaps had served together in the Gulf or Somalia—maybe even Lebanon or Vietnam. Hell, wherever the term came from she knew she'd probably never really know. Still, she couldn't resist.

"I've been meaning to ask you something," she said, turning to face Cooper. For the first time, she noticed the quivering man huddled in the darkened corner of the chopper. He was bound and gagged.

MacEwan decided not to even ask about the prisoner, and instead continued with her train of thought. "Why does he keep calling you 'Sarge'?"

The Executioner smiled, shook his head and stared out at the passing night.

* * * * *

Don't miss the exciting conclusion of
The Carnivore Project.
Look for The Executioner #320
Exit Code *in July.*

TAKE 'EM FREE
2 action-packed novels plus a mystery bonus

NO RISK
NO OBLIGATION TO BUY

MAELSTROM

The fuse of a new global war is lit on America's streets....

An advanced weapon prototype is hijacked by an unidentified group of mercenaries and followed by a wave of massacres in the streets of America's cities. The torch of anarchy and hatred has been lit, and waves of destruction have begun to spread across the globe. A crisis has erupted as angry radicals are poised to become deadly freedom fighters so powerful that not even the superpowers can oppose them. Stony Man's only chance...America's only chance...is to strike first, strike hard, strike now....

STONY MAN®

*Available
August 2005
at your favorite retailer.*